BRACE FOR IMPACT

Nuclear Survival: Southern Grit Book One

HARLEY TATE

BRACE FOR IMPACT

Nuclear Survival: Southern Grit Book One

What if an EMP is only the first strike?

With a credible threat to the United States and a plane stuck on the tarmac, Grant Walton is thirty seconds from full-blown panic mode. He's the only one in the airport who knows the truth. When the power goes out, he can't waste another second. It's the beginning of the end and every man for himself.

A nuclear attack will rip the country apart.

Leah Walton is wrapping up a twelve-hour shift as a nurse in the heart of the city. When the power goes out, the hospital operates on crisis mode. She can't stop to breathe, let alone check her messages. When she finally listens to her husband's frantic calls, she's faced with an impossible choice: leave or die trying.

Could you drop everything to save yourself?

Grant and Leah race the clock to find each other

before the United States is plunged into chaos. When the bombs fall, their worst fears come true. Can Grant make it home in time to find his wife? Will Leah escape the brunt of the blast?

The EMP is only the beginning.

Brace for Impact is book one in *Nuclear Survival: Southern Grit*, a post-apocalyptic thriller series following ordinary people struggling to survive after a nuclear attack on the Unites States plunges the nation into chaos.

Subscribe to Harley's newsletter and receive *First Strike*, the prequel to the *Nuclear Survival* saga, absolutely free.

www.harleytate.com/subscribe

CHAPTER ONE

GRANT

Charlotte International Airport
   Charlotte, North Carolina
   Friday, 4:30 p.m., EST

Grant leaned over and caught the flight attendant's eye as she walked up the aisle. "Excuse me, is there a status update?"

Her face glazed over in an empty smile. "I'm afraid not."

"How about phones? I need to make a call."

Her cheeks rounded. "I'm sorry, but as long as we are on the tarmac and away from a gate, we cannot allow the use of electronic devices." Her face melted into a mask of calm as she walked away.

Grant forced an exhale. When he paid to change his flight to the first departure available, he assumed the airline meant it. Now he sat on the asphalt outside the airport, ticking time off his watch and still no closer to home. He balled his hand into a fist and punched the tray table in front of him.

The woman in the seat exclaimed as he pulled his hand away. A knuckle-shaped dent remained.

Grant threw up an apology. "Sorry. Slipped."

"You all right, buddy?" The man sitting in the only other occupied seat in his row eyed Grant with a mix of concern and irritation.

"Fine." He flexed his hand and focused on the ache from the punch. Maybe he would make it off the plane without causing a scene.

The woman in front of him stood up. Maybe not.

She waved her arm and hollered toward the flight attendant. "Excuse me! Excuse me! I need some help."

Grant shifted in his seat. He refused to be taken off the plane for a punch that hurt no one. He'd had kids kick the back of his seat for hours and they were never forced off the plane.

Someone else behind Grant spoke up. "We've been waiting for hours. You can't keep us prisoner!"

Another voice from farther back called out. "Yeah! Let us use our phones or let us off the plane!"

If I'd rented a car, I'd be halfway home by now. Instead, he was stuck in Charlotte, staring out the airplane window at a stand of pine trees, unable to call his wife or anyone else.

He'd started his day like any other business trip: a cup of coffee, a glance at the news, and a stroll through the aisle of the ballroom-turned-conference. WelSoft paid him to scope out hacker tournaments all over the country and ensure their software passed with flying colors. If none of the hackers managed to bypass WelSoft's multiple layers of security and break into the backend of their consumer retail products, Grant had a good day.

Ordinarily, today would qualify, but instead of finding a fatal flaw in a WelSoft product, a pair of college kids stumbled on a threat to the entire United States: a coordinated attack involving nuclear weapons and the top twenty-five major cities, including Atlanta, Grant's hometown.

At first he thought they were crazy, but after watching them run away one after the other like scared kids in a horror movie, he couldn't ignore the possibility. After telling his boss to shove it, Grant headed straight for the airport.

All he kept thinking was what if he knew and did nothing? What if he let his wife die in the worst attack on American soil since the Civil War while he sat in a hotel in Charlotte, a few hundred miles away?

Grant glanced at the woman still standing up in front of him. *Hell with it.* He unbuckled his seat belt and stood up. Sitting and waiting wasn't an option anymore. He had to get out of there. He had to get home to his wife.

"What are you doing?"

"I'm getting off this plane."

"They'll arrest you."

Grant glanced down at the man beside him. Portly, with a belly hanging over his jeans and a golf shirt with the logo of The Masters above his heart. Grant scrubbed his face. "I'm only on this flight because of a family emergency. I have to get home."

"You won't do it by making a scene. They'll haul you into one of those little rooms in the airport and you won't get out for hours." The guy lowered his voice. "And that's only after the strip search."

"How do you know?"

He swallowed. "I complained to the agent running the x-ray machine. I thought she should pay more attention to the bags than her TSA boyfriend."

"Ouch."

"Tell me about it. I couldn't walk straight for a week."

Grant snorted out a laugh and a dose of pent-up tension fled his body. He needed to leave, but barging into the aisle might not be the best approach.

As he ran a hand through his hair, the loudspeaker crackled.

"Thank you for your patience, ladies and gentlemen. It appears our plane is experiencing a mechanical difficulty that cannot be repaired. In a moment, we will be towed back to the gate where you will deplane. Another aircraft is waiting for you and we will depart as soon as we can migrate you over."

The plane burst into a cacophony of angry chatter and shouts. Grant eased back down into his chair.

"Guess today is your lucky day."

Luck didn't begin to describe it. He held his phone in his hand, waiting. The plane lurched forward and he watched out the window. The second the gate touched the exterior, he turned on his phone and placed a call.

His wife's voicemail picked up again. Grant hit end and pinched the back of his neck. Not being able to talk to Leah was clouding his judgment. All he could see was her face. All he could hear were her screams when a bomb went off.

He checked his watch—4:45 p.m. She would be ending her shift at five. Fifteen more minutes, then she would head for her locker, find her phone, and call. He just needed to hold on until then.

The door to the plane opened and everyone inside the cabin stood up. Grant waited his turn behind businessmen and college kids and families on vacation. A sea of haggard faces and headaches. Bad tempers and aching backs.

As he exited the plane, he caught the flight attendant's eye. "Do you know when the next plane is leaving?"

"As soon as everyone is boarded and seated, we will get in line for takeoff. Hopefully an hour."

Grant thanked her and strode toward the terminal. He couldn't wait an hour, sitting on his hands doing nothing. He would lose the little sanity he had left.

While a pair of airline employees waved everyone over to a new line across the terminal, Grant turned the other way. The sign for ground transportation pointed straight ahead and Grant followed it.

Forget planes. He would rent a car.

Following the signs, Grant hustled through the

airport, filtering out the chatter from fliers as he passed. He bobbed and weaved through throngs of people waiting to board flight after flight. The airport was at capacity, with thousands of people leaving Charlotte and heading all over the country.

He wondered if they would make it home before hell broke loose. *Will I?*

Ground transportation occupied the lower level and Grant quickened his step toward the escalator. He waited for a man with an oversized suitcase to finagle it on board before following a few paces behind. The escalator creaked and groaned as it descended and Grant checked the time. Five o'clock.

As he reached again for his phone, the entire escalator shuddered. The lights above his head shut off. The woman behind him stumbled forward as the stairs stopped moving. He caught her by the shoulders.

"I'm sorry!"

"Are you okay?"

She backpedaled and pushed a wave of curls off her forehead. "I think so. That's what I get for texting while riding, isn't it?"

Grant nodded and turned back around. People were righting themselves and climbing down off the escalator in front of him. Their heads swiveled as they spoke to their neighbors.

The man with the huge suitcase struggled down each stair. Grant bit his tongue. No good would come of causing a scene.

While everyone filed off the escalator ahead, the man

and the suitcase ambled down one stair at a time. *Thunk. Thunk. Thunk.* Grant followed at a snail's pace, chewing on his cheek to keep his temper in check.

At last, they reached the bottom and Grant raced around the struggling man. He came to a stop in the middle of baggage claim. The airport was dark. Not a single light, emergency or otherwise, lit up the space. The baggage carousels sat still and motionless. No sound of air-conditioning or mechanical processes.

There were only voices echoing off the silent, unlit walls. People flocked to the only source of light—the giant, floor-to-ceiling windows to the outside. A handful gathered at the automatic doors, trying in vain to pry them open. A baby wailed in the distance.

Grant pulled out his phone and dialed his wife again. *Fast busy signal.*

He shot off a text and waited for the little blue line to finish its trek across the screen. A red exclamation point showed up instead. *Undeliverable.*

Grant shoved the phone in his pocket. *Was this it? Did it already happen? Am I too late to save her?*

A million questions rapid-fired in his brain and Grant spun around in a circle, his small carry-on suitcase still in his hand. Sweat beaded on the top of his brow and he came to a stop in front of the still-shut automatic doors.

He didn't know what happened outside the airport, if this was the end or only the beginning, but there was only one way to find out.

CHAPTER TWO
LEAH

Georgia Memorial Hospital
  Downtown Atlanta
  Friday, 4:30 p.m.

Leah wiped the back of her hand across her forehead and smeared her sweat and makeup. It had been a hell of a day. As soon as she got home, she would throw on her pajamas, open a bottle of wine, and put her feet up.

If only starter homes way outside the city came with masseuses on call. She palmed her hips and took a breath. Only thirty minutes left. *I can do this.*

"Am I going to be all right?"

Leah smiled down at the elderly woman lying on the bed beside her. "You're going to be fine, ma'am. Your vitals are reading normal and your blood sugar is dropping."

"I'm still light-headed."

Leah nodded. "It's the insulin. We had to give you a pretty big dose. Next time you go out for lunch, you need to remember to take your medicine."

"I don't know how I missed it this time. I always put it in my purse."

"Maybe you should carry some extra, just in case."

The woman nodded and closed her eyes as Leah's pager buzzed. She excused herself from the patient and rushed to room eight.

A doctor stood beside a bed, needle in one hand, the other wrapped tight around the wrist of a pediatric patient. The little girl couldn't have been older than ten, with dark brown hair and a nasty case of the freak-outs.

The doctor's voice hovered below a shout. "I said hold her down!" Leah gave a start. If Doctor Phillips was yelling, then it was serious. The man never raised his voice.

"She's not cooperating!" Rebecca, the nurse attempting to control the child, held one leg and struggled to grasp the other. The child kept aiming her foot at Rebecca's face.

Leah rushed up to help, grabbing the free leg and holding it down while the child whipped back and forth on the bed. "What's going on?"

Rebecca explained. "She came in complaining of shortness of breath. We gave her a breathing treatment and it didn't do any good."

The patient launched herself up from the middle of

the bed in a near-perfect imitation of the child in *The Exorcist* and Leah lost her grip on the ankle. Before she could get it back, she suffered a solid kick to her shoulder. Leah groaned and grabbed the patient's thigh. "Then what?"

"Then I brought out the needle." The doctor leaned over and jabbed the needle into the meaty area an inch above Leah's hand. The kid howled, but as soon as the doctor stepped away, she stopped kicking.

Leah let go and exhaled. The patient sucked in a breath, struggling to get any air. Her little chest heaved again and again.

"Will she be all right?"

"If she stops throwing a fit and lets the steroid do its job, hopefully. But if she keeps riling herself up, all bets are off. Her lungs are seizing and refusing to let in enough oxygen."

Leah nodded. She'd seen patients like this before. When some people couldn't breathe, they panicked, which closed their airways and compromised their breathing. It was a vicious cycle that could end in traumatic injury or death.

As she watched the little girl struggle, Leah rubbed her shoulder. It would bruise something fierce.

Rebecca reached out a soothing hand to the child and stroked her hair. "Work on slow, steady breaths. In and out. One, two, three, four..." The girl sucked in a rattling breath and exhaled. Rebecca smiled. "There we go."

Leah exhaled in relief and stepped back. Exhaustion

wobbled her knees and she reached for the doorframe, barely managing to stay upright.

"You need a break, Walton?" Dr. Phillips smiled at her as he monitored the child's breathing on the computer screen beside the bed.

"My shift's almost over. It's been a long day."

"Tell me about it. I've been here since yesterday."

Leah didn't envy residents. Thirty-six-hour shifts with only cat naps for sleep didn't seem fair. How could someone be expected to give the best care when they were running on fumes? She knew at the end of a grueling twelve hours, she didn't give a hundred percent. She couldn't imagine what it must be like for Dr. Philips.

She waved goodbye to Rebecca and stepped into the hall.

"Busy shift, huh?" Brandy smiled as she stopped beside Leah. Three years her senior at the hospital, Brandy earned her choice of shifts, but she still opted for three twelve-hour stints a week.

Leah nodded. "It's been crazy. First that car crash on Maple, then the house fire. And all the regulars." She wiped her forehead again.

"Flu season's a beast and it's not even peaked yet."

"I heard Augusta's run out of beds."

"No." Brandy looked at her with wide eyes. "Are they turning people away?"

"I don't know. But if anything else happens around here, we'll have to."

Brandy poked her in the arm. "Don't even think it.

We're the biggest hospital in town. If we turn people away, where will they go?"

Leah shook her head. "Forget I said anything. It's just the tired talking."

"Are you too tired for news?" Brandy grinned while biting her lip.

"What?"

"Twelve weeks today."

Leah scrunched up her nose. *Twelve weeks?* All at once it clicked and she wrapped Brandy up in a hug. "Congratulations! I know you and Travis have been trying for a while."

Brandy nodded. "Almost a year. We waited until everything checked out to tell anyone, but I'm going to be a mom!"

Leah couldn't be happier for her friend. Brandy would be a great mother. It was all she ever talked about since her husband finished school. Leah glanced at the floor. Once she finished the ER rotation, Leah hoped to start a family of her own. Soon, but not now.

She lifted her head with a smile. "Are you going to find out if it's a boy or girl?"

"I want to, but Travis doesn't."

Leah listened while Brandy gushed about her husband and the baby and potential names until her pager went off again. She pulled it off her belt. *The nursing station?* Leah shrugged and smiled at her friend. "Gotta go."

She hustled to the station and leaned against the counter. "Leah Walton. Someone paged me?"

The assistant behind the counter nodded. "Your husband called the main line and asked you to call him right away. Sounded pretty urgent."

Leah frowned. "Grant Walton, are you sure?"

"That's what he said."

"Thanks." Leah spun around, confusion battling the tiredness in her bones. *Grant called the main line?*

Her husband never called her at work. He knew how crazy her shifts were and didn't want to interrupt. If he called, something must have happened. An accident? Something with his mom?

Leah headed toward the lockers when a voice called out. "Nurse? Can you assist?"

She backpedaled and stuck her head in the room. Dr. Simpson stood hunched over a patient with one hand holding a suture and the other a bloody sponge. Leah rushed up to his side and took the sponge.

"Thanks." The doctor smiled at her. "This one's a bleeder."

She grabbed a new sponge and tore it open before changing it out for the saturated one. Harry Simpson was one of the new batch of residents they received last month. Definitely one of the greener ones. She smiled at him. "I heard you did a great job with the chest pains patient yesterday. You saved his life."

"Thanks." Simpson finished up the suture and stepped back.

The patient focused on Leah. "Will there be any scarring?"

She shook her head. "Not with Dr. Simpson's fine stitches. Give it a few weeks and you won't see a thing."

Simpson cut her a glance, but said nothing.

"I'll clean up." Leah smiled. "I'm sure you have more rounds."

"Thanks." The doctor left and Leah tended the patient's wound, cleaning the surrounding area before applying a clean bandage.

"Did that guy really know what he was doing?"

Leah glanced down. The patient looked about twenty, with a prior break to his nose and a scar along his chin. "You have experience with stitches?"

"Maybe a few." He grinned. "Happens in football."

"I can imagine. And yes, Dr. Simpson knew what he was doing." Leah finished cleaning the patient and stepped back. "Good luck with your healing. I hope you stay out of the ER for a while."

The patient smiled and Leah slipped into the hall. Every minute that went by not being able to call Grant added to her stress. Was he okay? Did something happen in Charlotte?

If no one else flagged her down, maybe she could finally make it to her locker to call her husband. She rushed down the hall and into the employee breakroom. Lockers lined the far wall and she beelined straight for hers on the bottom row. As she crouched to spin the combination lock, the lights flickered.

Leah tugged on the lock and swung open the door as the lights went out. *What the?* She shook her head. *Do the backup generators not power the breakroom?* It made sense if she thought about it. She fished for her phone in the dark, rooting past her street clothes and shoes for her purse. She tugged it open and found the phone.

As she pulled it free, Leah pushed the home button and the screen lit up, full of messages. She read the first one and almost dropped the phone.

CHAPTER THREE

GRANT

Charlotte International Airport
  Charlotte, North Carolina
  Friday, 5:30 p.m.

A series of dim lights flicked on overhead and the automatic doors to the airport slid open like molasses coated the gears. People flooded out into the dusk, relieved to be outside the confines of the dark and stagnant airport.

Grant hung back as a loudspeaker stuttered.

"Attention. This is the Charlotte International Airport Security Department. A widespread blackout is affecting a majority of the Charlotte metropolitan area. Our emergency backup generators are powering essential services and lighting only."

The speaker crackled as if the announcer covered the mic with his hand. After a moment, he returned. "All flights are currently canceled. Please remain calm and see the nearest flight attendant for assistance."

As soon as the word "canceled" came over the speaker, a collective groan rose up from the airport. A man five feet from Grant spun around in a circle, gesticulating and cursing. Another stormed toward the oversized baggage office, his fists coiled and muscles tight. Grant didn't want to be on the other end of that guy's vengeance.

A gaggle of angry passengers collected at the open doors.

"This is ridiculous! I've got to get home!"

"I've got to get to work!"

"My boss is gonna kill me!"

People were complaining and shouting and throwing up their hands. If airport security didn't show a bit of force, and soon, a mob would form. Grant didn't want to be there when that happened.

He spun around. A bank of rental car companies sat in the dark a hundred feet from where he stood. Lines already stretched to the windows. It would take hours to get a car, if they even had any left by the time he reached a desk.

As he ran a hand through his hair, Grant looked around. There had to be a way to get out of there that didn't involve a plane or waiting in one of those lines. He exhaled as a sign caught his eye

Additional Rental Car Facilities
Accessible via Shuttle

Bingo. Grant exhaled in relief. He could hop a shuttle and make it to a distant lot before most people figured it out. Easing around the mass of fliers still congregating by the doors, he slipped outside.

There had to be a sign for the shuttle somewhere. He squinted into the distance, eyeing all the cabs parked in the taxi stand. *How much for a taxi to Atlanta?* More than the money in his wallet, that's for sure.

He hustled up to the first cab where a driver leaned against the hood and smoked a cigarette. "You know where the rental car place is? The one with the shuttle?"

The man shrugged and spit out a bit of tobacco.

Grant moved onto the next driver and then the next. A man three cabs down with a beater of a car waved him over. "I know where it is."

"Great. Where?"

The driver pushed off the side of his car. "Ten bucks, I'll take you there."

"Ten bucks? How far is it?"

"A mile, maybe two. It's in a far lot at the edge of the airport."

Grant cursed under his breath. He could set off on foot, but without a clue as to where the office could be, it might take hours to reach it. By then, whoever was working would probably be long gone. It was either the cabbie or he tried his luck back inside.

With a scowl, he fished out a ten-dollar bill from his wallet and handed it over. It left him thirty-seven dollars and the emergency hundred tucked in the back. *Not nearly enough. I should carry more cash when I travel.*

The cabbie took the money and walked around the front of his car. It was a Crown Vic of dubious vintage. It had to be older than Grant himself. With a police headlight still attached to the front, it probably wasn't even legally licensed to be a cab. Grant shrugged it off. He didn't care as long as it got him to the rental place as quickly as possible.

He opened the rear door and clambered in with his suitcase. The cabbie eased into the front seat and the shocks squeaked. His dark brown eyes flashed in the rear view. "You from here?'"

Grant found the seat belt as the driver pulled away from the curb. "No. Atlanta. I'm trying to get home."

"Flight delayed?"

"I think they're all canceled. The airport's computers are down."

The cabbie whistled. "I wondered why we stopped getting fares. I've been sitting out there for twenty minutes."

While the cabbie talked about the airport and the power outage, Grant looked out the window. Not a single car passed them on the road. His brows knitted. Surely people were trying to pick up loved ones or were arriving without knowing the airport was shut down. Where was everyone?

They pulled out of the airport roundabout and onto a small exit road. A man stood by the side of his car, shouting at someone in the passenger seat.

The cabbie shook his head. "Some people. They are terrible fliers."

Grant nodded. The farther they drove in the dark without a single streetlight to light their way, Grant's concern grew. The cabbie was taking him to the rental car place, right? Grant jerked his head toward the front seat. "You know where you're going, right?"

"Of course. It's just down here."

Grant exhaled, but he couldn't slow the pounding of his heart. *Why did I get in the car?* It was stupid. He thought about all the other options. Walking, waiting at the airport, sweet-talking some airport personnel into bumping up his departure.

There were a million options, none of which involved getting in this guy's cab and leaving the relative security of the airport behind. Grant didn't know a damn thing about Charlotte. For all he knew, they were a stone's throw from the worst possible part of town.

He gripped the handle on his suitcase and stared out the window into the dark. The cab cruised along a two-lane road. From the glow of the headlights, he could make out an occasional blocky building like a warehouse, but that was all.

I can't stay in this car. I have to get back to my wife. Grant reached for the door handle as the cab slowed and turned right. It bounced over a speed bump and a yellow sign caught the headlights.

Car Rental Facilities

Grant exhaled. The cab driver was telling the truth.

He chastised himself for thinking the worst as the cab came to a stop in front of a small office building.

The cabbie put the car in park and craned his neck toward Grant. "You need help with your bag?"

Grant shook his head. "No. Thanks for the ride." He eased out of the back seat and shut the door with a wave.

The cab backed up, floating on ancient shocks, and headed back into the night. Grant turned around and walked up to the office door.

He tugged it open and a bell above his head jingled. He half expected a massive line, but he was the only customer inside. A single employee stood behind the counter with a flashlight pointing straight up to light the space.

The air hung thick and stale and Grant coughed.

The woman behind the counter called out, strain obvious in her voice. "I'm sorry, our computers are down. I can't retrieve your reservation."

He stepped forward despite the warning. Getting a car was his only option. He wouldn't leave until he did. "Lucky for me, I don't have a reservation."

She shook her head. "I can't take credit cards or pay via phone, either."

Grant reached the counter and the employee's features came into focus. She wasn't much older than him, maybe forty, with dyed blonde hair and dark circles under her eyes. The flashlight accentuated her makeup and made her almost ghoulish. He smiled.

"I'm happy to pay cash. Do you have anything available?"

"I don't know if I should." She smoothed her hair behind her ear. "We do everything over the computer. I won't be able to sync your reservation with the rest of our offices. It won't be in the system if you get in an accident."

Grant reached into his back pocket and pulled out his wallet. He fished out the hundred-dollar bill he kept for emergencies and smoothed it out on the Formica. "I only need a one-day reservation. Whatever you can give me for a hundred dollars cash."

The woman stared at the money, her brow knitting as she thought it over.

Please, just say yes.

Her frown deepened and Grant knew he was losing.

He leaned closer to read her name tag and tried again. "Darlene, I've got to get home. My wife is at the hospital. Please."

Her eyes flicked up to meet his. "Is she dying?"

"I don't know." Grant hated to lie. So far everything he'd said had been a version of the truth. "But I'll never forgive myself if I don't get there in time. Please." He pushed the money closer to her waiting hand.

Darlene stared at the money as she drummed her painted fingernails on the counter. At last, she snatched it from Grant's hand. "I shouldn't be doing this. I don't even know what cars are already reserved."

Grant exhaled in relief. He would get a car. He would make it in time. "I don't care what it is, anything that runs will be fine."

After slipping the money under the counter, Darlene

turned to face the board of keys. She shined the flashlight across the dangling tags. "Economy or intermediate?"

"Doesn't matter."

She plucked a set of keys from the second row and turned around. "Chevy Impala, then. Nobody likes to rent them. Too big and hard to steer."

Grant kept his comment to himself, and took the keys with a smile. "Thank you."

Darlene pointed at the lot with the flashlight. "It's in space number eighty-three. Do you need a flashlight?"

Grant shook his head. "No. I can manage. Thanks."

With his suitcase in one hand and the keys in the other, Grant hustled out of the office and down the rows of cars, searching in the dark for a Chevrolet Impala that would be his ticket home. He found parking spot eighty-three and almost whooped for joy.

The boat of a car took up the whole space and his suitcase seemed dinky inside the massive trunk. Grant slid into the driver's seat and shut the door. Silence enveloped him. He took a deep breath, stuck the key in the ignition, and turned it.

Nothing happened.

He frowned and tried again. Still nothing.

No matter how many times he cranked the ignition and pumped the gas, it was hopeless. The car wouldn't start.

CHAPTER FOUR

LEAH

Georgia Memorial Hospital
  Downtown Atlanta
  Friday, 5:30 p.m.

Twenty messages and a ton of voicemails, each one more urgent than the next. Grant wasn't making any sense. Leah scrolled through the messages, each one imploring her to leave the city and go to her sister's place.

Leah checked the time. *Five thirty on a Friday night?* It would take her two hours to reach Dawn's at least. Maybe more. Living outside of town had its advantages, but not when it came to rush-hour traffic.

She hit play on the most recent voicemail and listened to her husband's shaky voice. He sounded so upset. Afraid, even. What could have spooked him so bad? Why did he want her to leave?

She hit call on her phone, but it didn't go through. All

she got was a fast busy signal. She tried again. Same result.

She tried a quick text. *Not delivered!*

What the…? Everyone in the hospital must have been trying to call home. With thousands of cell phones all pinging off the nearest tower, it could be overwhelmed. She knew that sort of thing happened with 911 in a major catastrophe. A flood of calls would clog up the network and grind everything to a halt.

The backup lights for the hospital flickered on in the hall and Leah shoved her phone in her pocket. As she pushed the flyaway strands of her hair off her face, she stepped out of the breakroom and into chaos.

A nurse ran past her with a flashlight in her hand. A doctor shouted for help in a nearby room. The nursing station twenty feet away was a sea of bodies and raised voices. It didn't make sense. The hospital had enough generators to power all of the equipment for at least a week. Everything should have come back online almost instantly.

She hustled up to the nursing station. "What's happening?"

"What isn't?" The administrator held a hand to the top of her head as she struggled to stay calm. "The computers are fried. I can't log in. I can't check on anyone's vitals. Half the equipment in the rooms aren't working. The entire intensive care unit is beeping alarms."

Oh my God. Leah spun around. So many patients depended on the computer equipment to stay alive. In the emergency room alone there had to be twenty patients about to die.

As she rushed down the hall, a voice called out.

"I need any available nurses! Quick!"

She spun around. Kelly from the fifth floor stood at the stairwell waving a flashlight. Leah jogged to her. "What is it?"

Kelly grabbed her arm and tugged her toward the stairs. "The NICU. The incubators aren't working."

Leah's eyes went wide. "How many babies?"

"Ten." Kelly took the stairs two at a time and Leah followed. "We've got to get oxygen or they'll all die."

Leah thought fast. The incubators were all-in-one units supplying oxygen and heat and all the vital signs for the preemies. Without them, the nurses would need to cobble the same equipment together to make them work.

She paused on the landing. "The sixth floor has a bunch of manual oxygen tanks. They use them for the mobile COPD patients."

Kelly spun around. "Get them and meet me on five. Hurry."

Leah nodded, racing up the remaining flights, past Kelly who threw open the door to the fifth floor and on up to the sixth. She tugged on the door and stopped in the hall. Darkness enveloped her. *Where are the emergency lights?*

She stepped into the darkness. "Hello? Is anyone here?" *Damn it.* She didn't know where the oxygen tanks were located and without at least a little light, she would never find them in time. She threw open the first door. An empty room. The second was more of the same.

Cupping her hands around her mouth, Leah shouted into the dark. "Anyone! Please I need help!"

A single circle of light bobbed around the corner and came to rest at Leah's eye level. She shielded her face with her hand.

"Who is it?"

"It's Leah Walton from the ER. I need portable oxygen tanks for the NICU."

The light lowered and Leah blinked. Spots of gray and red floated before her eyes as the flashlight beam approached. "Sorry, the dark is freaking me out."

"Stacy?"

"Yeah."

"Thank goodness." Leah grabbed her arm. "Can you show me where the rolling oxygen tanks are? The incubators aren't working. We have ten babies that need to breathe."

"This way." Stacy hurried down the hall and opened a door. Inside sat an entire collection of oxygen. "I'll help get them downstairs."

"Thanks. What's going on? Where are the lights?"

Stacy shook her head. "Beats me. Maybe they turn off when it's an emergency?"

"The ER has backup lights."

"We're an outpatient floor. Everyone goes home by five. It's just me, an admin, and two other nurses."

Leah grabbed three tanks and hoisted them into her arms. They were heavier than she anticipated. She grunted and stepped into the hall. "See if the other nurses can help. We need to hurry."

Stacy grabbed two tanks and followed behind Leah, shouting as she entered the hall. "Lisa! Martine!"

Leah didn't wait. She huffed down the stairs, careful not to drop a tank, as footsteps sounded above her.

She set the tanks down to open the door, cringing at the delay. All the babies were suffering. She might be too late.

Grabbing the tanks, she rushed onto the floor. The commotion down the corridor caught her attention and Leah headed that way. The NICU was in full-on attack mode. Kelly and two other nurses rushed around, checking vitals on all the babies.

Leah set the tanks down. "I've got three and more are on the way."

Kelly looked up from one of the babies. "Hook them up. There are spare tubes on the far wall."

Leah didn't hesitate. She opened drawers and found the necessary equipment and readied the tanks for delivery. Another nurse she didn't know took two of the tanks as Stacy rushed in with two more nurses on her heels.

"We've got eight more."

"Bring them here, we can set them up." Leah ushered the women over and together they worked to hook up the oxygen and start the flow.

The NICU nurses took every tank as they finished, swapping out the breathing tubes of babies so small they made Leah shudder.

Kelly motioned to the wash station. "Can you scrub up? We need to keep them warm."

"What about warming blankets?"

"They'll all under stress. Skin-to-skin will work best."

Leah nodded. She knew even the littlest ones thrived on that kind of love. She scrubbed alongside Stacy while the other two nurses waited in line. In a matter of minutes, they had four warm bodies ready and eager.

Stacy ushered each woman to a chair and with delicate hands, moved the teeny preemies one at a time to waiting arms. Leah choked back a wave of tears. *So small.* The infant cradled in her left arm struggled with every breath, chest wobbling on an inhale, shuddering on an exhale.

She glanced up at Kelly. "Will they all make it?"

"I hope so. As soon as the power went out, we wheeled them all together. There's four oxygen tanks always in reserve here, but we're close to capacity at the moment. Hailey rigged up solo lines for our two most critical while Jen spliced the other line and increased the flow."

She exhaled and eased down into the only remaining chair with a single baby in her arms. "We'll see if it worked. Now if only the power would come all the way back on."

Stacy chimed in. "The sixth floor is totally dark. Not a single light."

Lisa from Stacy's unit agreed. "It isn't just the hospital, either. I looked out the window when the power went out. I can't see a single light that isn't a car."

"What?" Leah glanced up. "It's that big?"

Lisa nodded. "I think the whole city is dark."

"That's half a million people."

"If it's bigger than just the city limits, we're talking millions."

Kelly hung her head. "If all of Atlanta is in a blackout, we're about to get a heck of a lot busier. We need to get these babies stable without holding them. The rest of the hospital will need you."

The only nurse not holding a baby spoke up. "I'll go down to the ER and snag some warming blankets they use for hypothermia patients. We can cut them down to size and use them for the babies."

Kelly nodded as she thought it over. "We'll double up the smallest babies in the incubators, too. That will help maintain the temperature without having to hold them all."

Leah chewed on her lip as she stared down at the pair of sleeping babies in her arms. "What happens if the power doesn't come back online soon?"

Kelly hesitated. "We do the best we can. What other choice do we have?"

Leah thought about all of her husband's messages. The blackout was bigger than Georgia Memorial Hospital. Bigger than even the city of Atlanta. Whatever was happening out there, Leah feared the loss of power was only the tip of the iceberg.

CHAPTER FIVE

LEAH

Georgia Memorial Hospital
  Downtown Atlanta
  Friday, 8:oo p.m.

As Leah eased the last baby down into an incubator, a NICU nurse wrapped her in a warming blanket cut specifically for her size. The last few hours had given Leah a newfound appreciation for the nurses of the fifth floor. She could never care for a baby so tiny and vulnerable all day. She would lose her mind.

"You all right?"

Leah smiled at Kelly and nodded. "Just in awe of everything you do. That's all." She stepped over to the sink and lathered up her hands and arms. "I don't have the strength."

Kelly looked out over the room. Nurses stood at every incubator, manually checking vitals and oxygen levels.

"It's tough, but rewarding. When those little guys go home, it's worth it."

Leah swallowed. She hoped this time it would be that simple. "You think this is just a blackout?"

"Why wouldn't it be?"

"We've been dark a long time. Usually the hospital comes back online first." She dried her hands and pulled out her phone. "I haven't been able to make a call since we lost power. Have you?"

"Haven't tried." Kelly pulled out her own phone and tried to place a call. After a moment, she frowned and hit end. "All I get is a busy signal."

"Same here."

"Is anyone from the ER here?" A voice called out from the hallway and Leah turned. A member of the support staff stood with a clipboard and a flashlight.

Leah volunteered. "I'm from the ER."

Relief spread across the woman's face. "We need you back on one. We're at capacity and it's a bit crazy down there."

Leah walked toward the door. "At capacity? From what?"

"Car crashes."

"I don't understand."

"We can talk on the way. Come on." The woman motioned toward the hall and Leah followed.

She stopped at the doorway and turned back to Kelly. "Are you sure you're all right?"

"We're fine thanks to you. Go."

Leah nodded and jogged to catch up with the woman

from the ER. "Sorry. I was helping with the NICU." She held out her hand. "I'm Leah Walton."

The woman paused. "Wendy Clarkson. I work the night shift."

Leah smiled. "I only work days. Nice to meet you."

Wendy held the door open and Leah slipped into the stairwell. They hustled down side-by-side.

"Did you come in after the blackout?"

Wendy nodded. "It's chaos out there. When the lights went out, a ton of cars stopped working. Everything new just stalled out in the middle of the road."

"Are you serious?"

"Five crashes happened right in front of my bus. The old cars were still running, so they hit everything that wasn't. My bus still worked, but it couldn't get anywhere because the roads were jammed. I walked a mile to get here."

Leah exhaled. There was no way she could get to her sister's place north of town now. Forty miles might as well have been three hundred. She jerked her head up as another thought hit her. "What about ambulances and fire trucks? Are they working?"

Wendy shook her head. "Not any of the newer ones. We replaced our fleet a few years ago, so I'm sure they're toast. I'd bet some police cars still work. There's a lot of old ones still driving around."

Leah tried to piece it together. "How old are you talking?"

"Before cars turned into computers on wheels." Wendy glanced up at the ceiling as they hit the third floor. "I saw an old beater of a pickup still running. Maybe from the seventies? And a Buick like my grandfather used to have. Definitely a relic."

Leah swallowed down a wave of panic. "This doesn't sound like a typical blackout."

"You're telling me."

They hit the ground floor and Wendy paused with her hand on the push bar. "Are you ready for this?"

"That bad?"

Wendy nodded. "Most of the administration staff is gone. They left for the weekend before the blackout hit. No one's here to run anything."

"Crap."

"Worse." Wendy pushed the door open and the sounds of chaos blasted into the stairwell. "Help wherever you can for as long as you can."

"What about you?"

"I'll be at the main desk triaging incoming patients."

"Thanks." Leah watched Wendy hustle down the hall and she swallowed. Her shift ended hours ago. Other nurses were there to take her place. She knew Grant would want her to turn around and leave. Find some way to get out of the city and to her sister's place. But she took an oath to help people in need.

Patients lined the hallway on gurneys and in wheelchairs. One woman sat holding a bloody rag to her head. Another groaned and doubled over, clutching her stomach. Leah couldn't leave people like this. It was why she became a nurse.

But her husband and family needed her, too.

"Nurse, please. Come quick." A doctor in a bloodied lab coat waved at her from three doors down.

Leah walked on autopilot toward him. He ushered her inside a room where a man thrashed on the bed. A gash across his head dripped blood into his eyes, but it didn't seem to faze him at all. He gesticulated wildly, flinging his arms across his body again and again.

"You all are going to die! It's the end of the damn world and you're standing around like idiots! Run! Run! Run!"

Leah glanced at the doctor.

"Don't ask me. He was like this when he came in, ranting about *Apocalypse Now* and Armageddon." He turned to the patient and smiled. "It's just a blackout, sir. Now lie still so I can stitch up that cut."

"No!" The man jerked in the bed. "It's not a blackout! It's just the beginning. We've been attacked! Don't you get it? It's the start of World War III!"

Leah stepped closer and drew the patient's attention. "You mean like a bomb? Or air strikes?"

The man stopped flailing and turned toward her. His blue eyes widened as he calmed. "Worse. A high-altitude ballistic missile with a nuclear warhead attached."

"A what?" Leah shook her head as the man rattled off the same description again. "What is that? A nuclear bomb?" She *tksed*. "That's impossible. We'd all be dead."

The man leaned back and rested his head on the pillows. "Not at high altitude. When a nuclear explosion occurs hundreds of miles up in the atmosphere, it triggers a massive electromagnetic pulse. An EMP."

Leah bit her lip and watched from the corner of her eye as the doctor brought a side table and suture kit over to the patient's bed. The man had be a professor or one of those fringe types who spent all his time on the internet. Whichever, it didn't matter. As long as he talked to her, he didn't try to attack the doctor. She had to keep it going.

"I don't understand." Leah forced a helpless smile. "Can you explain it?"

The man lit up like she'd told him he'd won the lottery. "An EMP is a wave, like a radio wave, but full of energy. There are three different types. E_1, E_2, and E_3. Solar storms and space weather give off the E_3 type—it's a low, lumbering wave that will fry the power grid, but not much more."

The doctor leaned in and began to clean the wound. He motioned at Leah to keep the patient talking.

She stammered. "But I... uh... heard cars don't work."

"Exactly." The man didn't even blink when the doctor swiped numbing agent across his forehead. "That's why this isn't a natural blackout. High-altitude nuclear detonations release a massive E_1 EMP. Those will fry anything with a big enough computer. Most of the power grid, new cars, big computers. Smaller things like phones and watches and even some computers if they weren't plugged in will still work. But that's it."

Leah exhaled. Stitches were the only thing left. The doctor opened the suture kit and pierced the man's skin just above the gash. The patient flinched and Leah asked the first thing that came to mind. "When will it all come back on? Does the power company just reset it?"

He snorted. "It's not that simple. The EMP melted the wires and exploded generators. There's probably a million fires raging up and down the East Coast."

"What are you saying?"

The doctor finished the last stitch and the patient surged forward. "Enjoy the backup generators while they last. When they go out, that's all the electricity you're going to get."

Leah's mouth fell open. "You're joking."

"I wish I were. But an EMP like that wrecks everything in its path. The power won't be coming back on."

Forget keeping him talking, if what the man said were true, Leah needed to know more. "Do you know how widespread the blackout is? Is it just Atlanta?"

"I was sitting with my laptop trying to get on the web to find out when a sports car slammed into the bus stop. Lucky he didn't kill me."

Leah frowned. "I thought you said cars weren't working."

"His wasn't. The idiot put it in neutral and pushed it down the hill. He thought he'd catch up to it and ride it all the way down."

Whoa. "You're lucky to be alive."

"Tell me about it." The man smiled at the doctor. "Thanks for fixing me up."

The doctor nodded. "Thanks for not attacking me."

"Your nurse deserves that thanks. I was so wound up with what happened and the pain, I lost it there for a bit."

His eyes narrowed at the doctor. "Didn't help that no one would listen."

Leah pulled out her phone. "If I can get on the web, do you think there will be some news?"

"There must be, but I'm afraid you won't have any luck. There's too many people here all trying the same thing. The network can't handle this type of capacity."

She slid her phone back in her pocket. "What do we do now?"

The patient glanced at the door. "If I were you, I would get the hell out of the city. It'll only get worse from here on out."

CHAPTER SIX

GRANT

Rental Car Facility, Charlotte International Airport
Charlotte, North Carolina
Friday, 8:00 p.m.

Grant stared out the windshield into the darkness. *This can't be real.* He tried the key again, but nothing happened. With a groan, he pulled it from the ignition, got out, and retrieved his luggage. Darlene wouldn't be happy to see him.

He hustled back to the office and yanked on the door. It didn't budge. *Oh, no.* He stuck his face against the glass and cupped his hand around his eyes to see inside. No flashlight and no Darlene.

Did she leave? He stepped back and scanned the door for store hours—8 *a.m. to 8 p.m., Monday through Friday.*

Grant checked his watch. Five after eight. *Damn it.* She couldn't have gone far. No car lights lit up the lot and

Grant didn't hear any engines. He hurried around to the back and searched the lot for any sign of her.

One car sat in a parking spot behind the building, close to the rear entrance. A little Honda with bright red paint and a bubble butt. Movement inside caught his eye. *Darlene.* She banged on the steering wheel with both fists and her blonde hair fluffed in front of her face.

Grant hurried forward. She couldn't leave without him. He rapped on the driver's-side window. Darlene jerked in her seat and even with the windows rolled up, her scream pierced the night.

He held up his hands in apology and Darlene's shock gave way to irritation. She pushed open her door.

"Won't start?"

"No." She ran a hand through her hair and tamed the worst of it. "Which makes zero sense. This car is brand new."

"The rental wouldn't start, either."

Darlene's eyes widened as she looked up at Grant. "What? That's impossible. I drove that one earlier today."

Grant shrugged. "I tried everything."

Darlene leaned back in the seat. "What's going on? First the power, then the cars?"

"It's more than a blackout, that's for sure." Grant stepped back and Darlene eased from the car with her purse in one hand and useless keys in the other. "I have to get home. My kid's with a sitter. She charges for every five minutes I'm late."

Grant motioned to the office. "How about we try a few more cars? One of them has to work."

Darlene nodded and let Grant back into the office through the rear entrance. She turned on the flashlight she'd left by the door and together they picked out handfuls of keys.

Fifteen minutes later, they regrouped at the counter with a pile of discarded keys and no luck.

Darlene snuffed snot back into her throat. "My son is going to be worried sick. He never goes to bed until I tuck him in."

Grant pulled out his phone and tried to call his wife. Instead of the fast busy signal, a recording he hadn't heard in years played in a loop. *All circuits are busy. Please try your call again.* He shoved his phone back in his pocket with a frown. "Do you have any other cars? Anything else we could try?"

Darlene shook her head. "What's the use? They won't work." She palmed her forehead in exasperation. "How does every car stop working all at once?"

Grant gave a start. "It's not every car."

"What are you talking about?"

"I got here in a cab." Grant scanned his memory, trying to parse out the differences between the cab and the cars on the lot. He clapped his hands when he placed it. "It was old. A real beater. Late seventies, early eighties maybe. It didn't even have power windows."

Darlene chewed on a fingernail, wrecking the polish. "You think being old had something to do with it?"

"Had to." Grant thought it over. "Lack of computers, maybe? Cars were a lot simpler back then."

"How could a blackout fry the electronics in a car?"

"I don't know." He thought about what Baker told him so many hours ago standing outside the Charlotte airport. Could a nuclear bomb do this? Was he already too late?

I can't wait around here to find out. He turned to Darlene. "Got anything with a simple engine around here?"

She turned toward the windows and thought it over. After a moment, she answered with hesitation. "The daily lot probably does."

"They house rentals there?"

"No."

"I'm not following."

She pulled her lower lip between her teeth. "Lots of people park at the airport to take a flight."

Grant's eyes narrowed. "You mean we could steal one."

Her eyes cut to his face. "I was thinking more borrow, but yeah."

Grant pinched the bridge of his nose. *Steal a car?* He'd made a point of never breaking the law. Not even as a kid. He might have faked a stomach bug to get out of a test or lied when his mother-in-law asked if he liked dinner, but he'd never committed a crime.

"Stealing a car is a felony."

Darlene rubbed her eyes and smeared mascara onto her cheeks. "You're right. I wasn't thinking straight." She turned to look at the parking lot. "I just need to get home."

"Then I say we hike to the airport, see if we can find

another working cab. It might take a while, but we'll find one eventually."

She nodded. "All right. I know the way. As long as we stay on the road, we can get back to the airport even in the dark."

Grant picked up his suitcase and headed toward the back door when a shout stopped him still.

CHAPTER SEVEN

GRANT

Rental Car Facility, Charlotte International Airport
    Charlotte, North Carolina
    Friday, 10:00 p.m.

Grant grabbed Darlene by the shoulder and dragged her
down beneath the counter. He stole the flashlight from
her limp grip and turned it off.

"What are you doing?"

"Keeping us safe."

The shouts increased. "Look at all the cars on the lot!
They've got to have some that work!"

The front door jiggled. "Open up, damn it! We need
to get out of here!"

In the dark without the flashlight, Darlene wasn't
much more than a trembling shape beside Grant. He
shifted his weight on his heels. "We can wait this out.
Once they give up and leave, we can walk to the

daily lot."

More fists pounded on the glass and Darlene shuddered. "What if they don't leave?"

"Then we run for it."

"The only other exit is the back door."

"Is it secure?"

"It locks automatically."

"Good." Grant didn't want to be stuck in the office any longer than he had to, but not worrying about a mob rushing them from behind helped him focus. He'd dealt with angry jerks before both in the military and for WelSoft. Conferences could turn unruly when prizes were held back on technical grounds.

He'd had to break up more than one fight between a furious hacker and a company man. But that was one-on-one. Two at the most. He'd never faced a mob.

The shouts rose and fell outside as people tried the door again and again. They weren't giving up. A woman's voice carried over the dull rumbling. "Please, if you're in there, we need cars! We need to get home!"

"We have children!"

"Come on! We'll pay for a rental!"

Darlene shifted beside Grant, but he reached out and fumbled for her arm. "Don't."

"Those people sound desperate. I should at least tell them the cars don't work. Then they'll go away."

"It's not that simple."

"Of course it is. We don't have cars. Once they hear that, what can they do?"

"Lots of things." Grant held onto Darlene's forearm

with enough force to keep her from standing. "What did you suggest only a few minutes ago?"

Her answer came out hushed. "To steal a car that's running."

"Exactly. You think these people haven't thought the same thing? Aren't thinking it right now? Hell, I bet a few of them are trying to find a way inside."

Darlene shrank back. "You mean break in?"

"If you thought it was the only way to get home, wouldn't you?"

"I don't know..." She trailed off and Grant let go of her arm.

"We need to be ready to run. Do you know how to get to the airport without being seen?"

Darlene was silent for a moment. "I think so. If we go out the back, we can skirt along the cars and then take the access road into the parking deck. It's restricted access for vehicles. There's a crossing arm that's key card activated, but we can duck underneath it on foot. Then we cut through the deck and we'll be at the airport."

"Good. Do you have all your things?"

"My purse... I guess I can take the flashlight... I don't know what else."

Grant thought it over. "Is there a breakroom?"

"In the back."

"Food?"

Darlene exhaled loud enough for Grant to hear. "Some sodas and maybe a bit of stuff in the fridge."

"Grab everything and meet me by the back door in five minutes."

"What are you going to do?"

"Search for anything we can use." He turned toward the counter and used his fingers to feel across the shelves as Darlene scooted away into the back. Stacks of papers. A stapler. Nothing useful at all.

There had to be something. Grant turned around toward the back when he noticed the people outside weren't yelling anymore. He rose enough above the counter to risk a quick look out. A handful of lights glowed in the parking lot: cigarettes and cell phones.

Maybe they got tired of yelling and banging their fists on the glass. Grant doubted the angry mob was giving up. It was never that easy. He sneaked into the hall behind the counter and opened the first door. It was too dark inside to see a thing.

With short, sliding steps, he eased into the room. His foot hit something hard. A desk.

Must be the manager's office.

Grant worked his way around the slab of wood and wheeled out the chair before sitting down. One at a time, he rifled through the drawers, coming up with a handful of snack bars and what felt like a half-empty six-pack of Gatorade.

In the second drawer, he found a lighter and a pack of cigarettes. He added the lighter to the stack. In the top drawer, all he came up with was a box of paper clips, of which he pilfered a few.

Before he left the room, Grant pulled his wallet from his jeans and teased out what he hoped was a five-dollar bill. He set it on the middle of the desk, gathered his newfound items, and worked his way back to the hallway.

As he stepped through the doorway, he almost collided with Darlene. "What are you doing? I told you to wait at the back door."

"Why are you in Randall's office?"

Grant held up the food. "Gathering supplies. Don't worry, I paid for them."

"You shouldn't have. He's a jerk."

Grant snorted. "Too late. Did you find anything?"

Darlene held up a bag. "Six sodas and a pack of string cheese."

After adding his haul to the bag, Grant followed Darlene down the hall to the rear door. "You ready?"

"I guess. What do we do if someone's outside?"

As Grant opened his mouth to answer, a terrific crash stole his breath. The front window shattered to the floor as a brick skittered to a stop a few feet from his foot. He turned to Darlene. "We run. Come on."

Together, they busted out the rear door as shouts and whoops echoed down the hallway. Darlene pointed the way as Grant hoisted his suitcase in one hand and the bag of food in the other.

With Darlene in the lead, they rushed toward the line of parked cars and a modicum of cover. Angry airline passengers flooded out of the building behind them as Grant ducked behind a compact Toyota.

The lights from cell phones bounced all over the parking lot and Grant crouched low enough to hide behind the trunk. Darlene did the same three cars away. He hissed in her direction. "How far?"

"A hundred yards to the end of the row."

"Go." Grant followed Darlene's shadow as people shouted about makes and models of cars.

A car door slammed, followed by another, and another. The mob was gaining on them. Grant picked up the pace and the plastic bag of food crinkled as it bobbed in the air. By the time he reached the end of the row, his breath sawed in and out of his lungs.

Darlene could barely speak. "T-That way." She pointed parallel to the cars. In the moonlight, Grant could make out a yellow crossing arm.

"Is that the access road?"

Darlene nodded.

More shouts erupted behind them. "They don't work! None of them work!"

Someone laid on a horn. More glass shattered. It was turning into a riot. Grant tapped Darlene on the back. "Let's go."

They took off together, risking discovery to angle across the rest of the parking lot. Darlene ducked underneath the crossing arm and Grant followed. Neither stopped running until the lights bouncing around the parking lot were smaller than fireflies.

Grant clutched at his legs above the knees. "I need a minute." Too many days spent behind a desk and not enough miles on the treadmill. He heaved. "How far to the airport?"

Darlene huffed a few times before speaking. "At least a mile."

Ragged breaths sawed in and out of Grant's lungs, but he didn't have the luxury of recovery. He stood with a grimace and hoisted his suitcase off the ground. "All right. We won't get there standing around."

Grant took off and Darlene caught up after a moment, holding her shoes in her right hand. "I can't run anymore in heels."

They hurried the rest of the way in silence, ears open for any sound of an oncoming vehicle or an angry mob. By the time they reached the parking deck, sweat coated Grant's back and he'd been forced to stuff his jacket in his suitcase.

Darlene didn't fare much better. Her hairline was damp and she tied her suit jacket around her waist. Grant hated to think how the bottom of her feet fared.

She pointed at the deck. "We can snake through the daily lot and come out at the taxi stand."

Grant nodded.

"You really think there'll be a taxi left?"

Grant scratched at his head. "We can hope, right?"

They eased through the lot, moving around row after row of parked cars until the glow of lights stopped them still. Darlene ducked behind a sedan while Grant eased forward. The airport had devolved into chaos.

Thousands of people milled around outside, talking, smoking, pointing at the sky. Some even stood in the middle of the road, daring nonexistent cars to run them over.

"What's going on?" Darlene crouched beside Grant at the front fender of the car.

"Looks like no flights have taken off."

"The taxi stand is full of cars."

Grant frowned as he scanned the row of shiny, late-model vehicles. Not a single driver stood beside one waiting for a fare. "None of them are working."

Damn it. He had to get out of Charlotte, but without a working vehicle, he would never make it home. He ran a hand over his head and closed his eyes. There was only one option, even though he hated to use it.

Grant exhaled and turned to Darlene. "Let's find a car."

She blinked. "You mean to steal?"

"I was thinking more borrow, but yeah."

Darlene smiled and Grant couldn't help but smile back. She squared her shoulders. "Old, right? No computers inside?"

Grant nodded. "As old as we can find."

They split up, canvassing the parking deck in search of a vehicle that might still turn over. Grant spied one first. He let out a low whistle and waited.

Darlene tracked him down. "Find something?"

He pointed at a gold floater of a sedan with a grin. "A 1977 Oldsmobile Cutlass Supreme."

Darlene raised an eyebrow.

"First car I ever drove. This one's even got the spoke wheels." He walked over to it and tried the door handle. It didn't open.

Grant set his suitcase down and unzipped it. He

pulled out his suit and eased it off the hanger from the dry cleaners. He stared at the twisted piece of metal as he made his decision.

Darlene stood beside the car, waiting.

"You keep watch. It'll take me a minute to break in."

CHAPTER EIGHT

LEAH

Georgia Memorial Hospital
  Downtown Atlanta
  Saturday, 12:15 a.m.

Leah fell into a chair in the employee breakroom and chugged a bottle of water. For hours, she'd been torn between trying to find a way out of the city and helping as much as she could. So far, helping won out.

Dead on her feet, she didn't know how much longer she could work without collapsing. She closed her eyes and visions of a nuclear bomb exploding overhead shot them back open. Did a bomb really go off in the atmosphere?

Was that why cars and incubators and most of the hospital's equipment didn't work? Leah unwrapped a squished granola bar she found in the bottom of her purse and chewed in silence. What about radiation? Fallout? Did any of that matter?

She checked her watch. After midnight already. Leah had been working for nineteen hours.

"You look like I feel."

Leah twisted around in the chair. "That bad, huh?"

Dr. Phillips leaned against the lockers with an exhausted smile. "Thanks for helping with the pediatric patient earlier. Is your shoulder all right?"

My shoulder? Leah glanced down and remembered. "It's fine. I've helped so many patients since then I forgot all about it. Is the girl okay?"

"Should be. She was breathing on her own, so we discharged her a few hours ago." The doctor fished a pack of cigarettes out of his coat. "Want to take a break?"

She wrinkled her nose. "I don't smoke."

He focused on the pack with a frown. "I don't very often. But a day like today, all bets are off." He glanced back up. "You sure you don't want some fresh air? I'll stay downwind."

Leah pushed off the chair. The thought of cold air lifted her spirits. "Why not? I haven't been outside in hours." She tugged her coat from her locker and shoved her purse back inside before following Dr. Phillips toward the stairs.

They hiked up six flights and walked down the dark halls to the side entrance for the employee level of the parking deck. Dr. Phillips opened the door and a blast of chilly night air hit Leah in the face. She stepped out and the doctor followed.

He lit a cigarette and sucked in a massive drag. His shoulders fell in gratitude. "Gets me every time."

Leah walked over to the retaining wall and stared out at the city. She swallowed. Thanks to the millions of lights downtown, the sky usually glowed purple even in the middle of the night. Now all she saw was darkness below her and a billion stars above her.

The feeble backup lights of the hospital barely lit the sidewalk. As far as she could see, darkness reigned. Every now and then, some small hint of light caught her eye, but nothing like it used to be. Were those lanterns? Flashlights? Cars that still worked? She didn't know.

Dr. Phillips joined her and let out a low whistle. "If I didn't know any better, I'd say this is the end of the world."

Leah shuddered. "What makes you think it isn't?"

The doctor took another drag. "It can't be. We would have an alert on our phones or someone from the hospital would have said something. It's a blackout, that's all."

"What if it's bigger than that?" Leah thought about the man in the hospital and all the texts and messages from her husband. "What if the whole country's affected?"

"Impossible."

Leah hesitated. At last, she couldn't help herself. She needed someone to talk to. "A patient came in earlier. He claimed this was all due to a bomb."

"What kind of bomb?"

"A nuclear explosion high up in the atmosphere. He said it caused an EMP that knocked out the power grid and the cars. Basically everything that runs on electricity."

"My phone still turns on."

Leah shrugged. "Maybe the little stuff is too small to break?"

The doctor sucked on his cigarette and the end glowed. "That sounds crazy."

"I know, but why else would we still be without power? Why don't cars work?"

"Are you sure they don't? I heard an EMT say that earlier, but how do you know it's true?"

Leah nodded out at the dark. "Do you see any?"

"It's the middle of the night."

"With six million people in the metro area, there should be cars. Even at midnight."

"True." The doctor pulled the cigarette pack from his coat and fished out another one. He lit it off the end of the first. "You have any family, Nurse Walton?"

"A husband and a sister."

Dr. Phillips dropped the stub of the first cigarette on the ground and crushed it with his heel. "My wife has got to be worried sick. I haven't been able to reach her."

"Same here."

Leah turned around to face the parking deck. It was mostly full. She squinted into the dark. "What is that?"

The doctor turned around. "I don't know. Looks like a backup light over by the cell tower."

She glanced at him. "What cell tower?"

"Ever noticed all those antennae on the side of the building?"

Leah nodded.

"It's a cell tower. That's why we've always got service in the hospital. Most emergency facilities have one."

Leah pulled her coat around her as the light moved. "Is that a person?"

"Looks like it. He's probably working on the power supply trying to get service. Hospitals are first priority for the phone company."

"Can I have a cigarette and your lighter?"

"I didn't think you smoked."

"I don't."

The doctor handed both over.

"I'm going to check it out."

"Want me to come?"

Leah shook her head. "But if I start screaming, I expect a rescue."

Dr. Phillips chuckled. "I'll try my best."

Leah took off for the cell tower, easing around employee cars as she walked across the top floor of the parking deck. As she neared, a single man stepped into the beam of a portable flood light rigged up on the ground.

She called out. "You have a minute?"

The man jerked up, startled. "Sorry. I'm on the clock."

She stepped into the light and held up the cigarette and lighter. "I just want some information."

In the light, she could see he was mid-forties, maybe fifty, with a grizzled beard turning gray in the middle. Construction boots and a workman's jumpsuit covered up a fit frame. He considered for a moment before closing the distance.

Leah held out the cigarette and the man popped it in his mouth. She lit the end and stepped back.

The cigarette glowed and the man closed his eyes. "That sure hit the spot. Thanks."

"You're welcome." Leah waited as he took another drag. "You work for the phone company?"

"Sure do."

"Why don't we have service?"

"Because the grid is toast."

She smiled like she was embarrassed. "Explain it to me like I'm five."

The man chuckled. "Think of the power grid like a massive web of electric wires. They run out from hubs, generators, substations, and major stations, all over the city. Usually, when a generator blows or a substation goes out, electricity is emergency-routed around the problem and the power comes back on within minutes."

"But that didn't happen this time."

"No." The man took another puff before continuing. "This time, something massive knocked the power out for the entire East Coast."

Leah stared, wide-eyed. "It's true."

He froze. "What is?"

"I had a patient come in ranting that a bomb went off in the atmosphere and took out the power grid."

"I believe it. They aren't saying much at headquarters, but from what I've seen, it makes sense."

"Care to elaborate?"

He shrugged. "Most cell towers aren't working. The large ones have backup generators that are supposed to kick on when the power goes out. Some are fried so bad, the generator won't turn on. Others are damaged and only half-working."

"Is that why calls won't go through?"

"Mostly. We have a few towers functional, but so many people are trying to call or get on the web that the system is overloaded. It's blocking most calls."

Leah perked up. "But some go through?"

"Some."

She exhaled. Maybe if she kept trying, she could finally connect with Grant. "When will the grid be repaired?"

He shook his head. "It's not that easy. If the entire East Coast is like Atlanta, I'd say years."

Her mouth fell open. "I'm sorry, I think I just hallucinated. Did you say years?"

"Afraid so. This isn't an easy fix. If the substations are damaged or even most of the generators, the power companies don't have the capacity to fix them." He pointed at the equipment behind him. "Even if I get this backup generator running, it's only got fuel for eight hours. Once the fuel runs out, if the power doesn't come back on, that's it. No more calls."

Leah blinked. no power for years? She couldn't process it. All she could do was try to work with what she had in the moment. She squinted up at the group of antennae in the dark. "Why are you here working? If it's hopeless, what's the point?"

The dropped his spent cigarette with a smile. "So a pretty girl can give me a smoke."

Leah blushed in the dark. "If you get this tower online, will I be able to make a call?"

"Maybe. It'll depend on how lucky you are."

She exhaled and took a step back. "Thank you for the information."

As she turned to leave, the man called out. "Who do you need to call?"

She looked back. "My husband."

The man fished something out of his jumpsuit pocket. "I've got a satellite phone. If you keep it short, you can make a call."

Leah's chest swelled with breath and hope. "You mean it?"

He nodded and held it out. Leah took the oversized phone and punched in Grant's number. It rang and rang. She crossed her fingers. It went to voicemail.

She tried to keep the disappointment out of her voice. "Hi baby, it's me. I hope you're somewhere safe. I'm still downtown, but don't worry about me. I'll be heading to Dawn's place as soon as it's light. Love you. Stay safe." She hung up and handed the phone back. "Thanks."

"No problem."

Leah rolled up on her toes. "Come the morning, if the grid isn't operational, what happens?"

The man rubbed his beard. "Things get a hell of a lot worse."

Leah thanked him again and turned around. She hustled back to Dr. Phillips.

"I was about to send in the cavalry."

She smirked. "And who would that be?"

"Hadn't figured that out quite yet." The doctor nodded toward the cell tower. "What did he say?"

Leah filled him in.

"Christ."

"Unfortunately, I don't think he's coming."

"What are you going to do?"

Leah stared out at the night. "As soon as daylight comes, I'm leaving. I promised my husband I'd meet him at my sister's place up north." She glanced at Dr. Phillips. "What about you?"

"The same. My wife must be out of her mind." He walked toward the stairwell and tugged the door open. "Maybe we can go together."

CHAPTER NINE

GRANT

Rental Car Facility, Charlotte International Airport
Charlotte, North Carolina
Saturday, 1:00 a.m.

It took longer than Grant expected to pop the lock on the Cutlass. He blamed rust—on the parts and his skill. Once inside, he slid back the driver's seat and leaned under the steering column.

This part he still remembered. In five minutes, he managed to pull out all the necessary wires, strip them, and tap the starter wires together. The car started on the second try.

Darlene stood beside the driver's door, shifting her weight back and forth on dirty bare feet. "How do you know how to do all this?"

Grant shrugged. "This is the same make and model as my first car. When I was a kid, I was always losing my keys. They'd be under my bed or in my backpack or somewhere. It was easier to strip the column and tap two wires together than find them."

"Didn't you worry about it getting stolen?"

Grant's eyebrows arched. "A '77 Cutlass? You're joking, right?'

Darlene surveyed the car. "You have a point."

"Get in. Let's hit the road before anyone hears us."

Darlene hustled around to the other side of the car before Grant backed the massive boat of a sedan out of the parking spot.

He paused in the aisle. "I have no idea where I'm going."

Darlene laughed and pointed. "Follow the exit signs. Then we'll get on the highway."

Grant did as she suggested, wheeling around the rows of parked cars, trying to stay as quiet as possible. He approached the exit and slowed. "Any trick to opening the gates without power?"

Darlene pointed. "Looks like that one is already broken."

On the far right of the exit, the crossing arm hung limp and shattered off the post. Grant eased toward it and sailed out of the parking deck. Darlene directed him toward the highway. As they drove past the airport, shouts filtered through the windows.

Grant checked the rearview. A handful of people ran after them, waving their arms. He watched as they grew smaller and smaller. Hopefully that was the last of angry mobs.

He turned onto the on-ramp for the highway and pushed the gas. As he approached highway speeds, Darlene shot her arm out. "Watch out!"

Grant slammed on the brakes. The highway was impassable. Cars littered the road. Some at awkward angles, some slammed into the rear of a car in front. Others just sitting in their lane like the owners parked and went to work.

"The power went out at five. Rush hour."

"So all of the cars on the highway..."

"Stopped working." Grant's breath caught as a man appeared in the beam of his headlights. He was running straight toward them. Soon another followed. Then a woman and a child.

"Help!"

"We need to get home!"

He turned to Darlene. "Is there another way to get to your place?"

She nodded. "We'll take back streets."

"Good."

Grant whipped the car in reverse and gunned it, squealing the tires as the first man came within a few feet. As Grant threw the car into drive, the man slammed a hand on the trunk.

Darlene screamed.

Grant punched the gas. The man faded into a cloud of dust and darkness. Only then did Grant exhale. Getting Darlene home would be a challenge, but he couldn't leave her in the middle of nowhere. She had a child.

As she pointed to a side street, Grant killed the headlights.

"What are you doing?"

"Not getting caught." He slowed to a crawl. "We're a target. As soon as people see the lights, they'll come running. We need to keep a lower profile."

As Grant's eyes adjusted to the moonlight, he picked up speed. "How far do you live?"

"Five miles."

Grant calculated in his head. At this rate, they'd make it in an hour, assuming all went well. He nodded. "Where do I turn?"

Suburbs of Charlotte, North Carolina
Saturday, 2:30 a.m.

The Cutlass eased over the curb and onto a driveway of a squat brick ranch. The curtains in the picture window fluttered.

"Thanks for driving me home."

"You're welcome." Grant stayed in the driver's seat while Darlene collected her purse and shoes.

She pushed open the door. "Aren't you coming?"

"Inside?"

"You need to eat and get a few hours of sleep."

"I don't want to impose."

Darlene stared at him. "You stole a car and navigated

through half of Charlotte in the dark. The least I can do is get you some food and a couch to sleep on for a few hours. You can leave for Atlanta in the morning when you can see what's coming."

Grant hesitated. Every hour meant that much longer before he could find Leah. But exhaustion would make him sloppy. Careless.

"Staying up all night won't do you any favors."

At last, he gave in. "You're right. Thanks." Grant pulled the circuit wires apart and the car shut off. After fishing his suitcase out of the back seat, he hurried to catch up with Darlene.

The front door opened before she could stick her key in the lock.

A girl of about nineteen or twenty stood in the entryway, one eyebrow about to take flight off her forehead. "Get stuck in traffic?"

"You don't want to know." Darlene pushed past her. "Liv, this is Grant. Grant, Liv."

Grant stuck out his free hand, but the girl only wrinkled her nose. "Nice car."

"Thanks." He followed Darlene into the kitchen. The woman was bent over a checkbook adding on her fingers. "I can pay you $150 now and the rest next week." She tore the check off the book and held it out.

Liv snatched it and read the amount. "That's it?"

"I'm sorry. I don't get paid until the end of the month."

"Fine. But just so you know, Mattie was worried sick. I had to bribe him with chocolate milk to get him in bed."

Darlene nodded. "Sorry."

Grant stood in the kitchen like a third wheel until the girl packed up her things and left. As the door shut behind her Grant spoke up. "Does she need a ride?"

"No. She bikes here. Lives a few streets over."

He nodded and shoved his hands in his pockets.

Darlene opened a cabinet and pulled down two glasses. "Bourbon or whiskey?"

Grant looked up. "Aren't they the same thing?"

Darlene pulled a bottle from the next cabinet over and poured two glasses. She handed one to Grant. "All bourbons are whiskeys, but not all whiskeys are bourbons. Depends on where they're made and what they're made of."

He took the glass and held it up. "I confess, I'm not much of a drinker."

Darlene smirked. "Obviously." She lifted her own glass. "To getting home before all hell breaks loose."

Grant clinked his glass against hers and took a sip. The amber liquid burned, but went down smooth. "Bourbon?"

She smiled. "Some of the best Kentucky has to offer. Although there's some good ones made in Georgia now, too."

While Darlene fished out a tea candle from a drawer and lit it, Grant took a moment to look around. The kitchen was small, but practical, with a farmhouse sink under the window and a range with a microwave above it on the far wall. Perfect for one person.

He took another sip of the drink and eased down into a kitchen chair. "So no husband?"

Darlene sat down opposite and crossed her legs. She rubbed one foot as she spoke. "No. He left when Matthew was only two. Claimed we stifled him, whatever that means."

Grant swallowed. If the blackout were only the start of whatever happened next, Darlene would have a tough time surviving. He glanced back toward the front of the house. "Do you have a basement?"

She tilted her head. "Partial, but it's not finished. Why?"

"If anything happens... If you see a flash of light or hear a boom, you need to take your son and get down there."

Darlene swallowed another sip of bourbon. "What are you talking about?"

Grant exhaled. "The blackout might only be the beginning."

"You're scaring me." Darlene got up and rustled through the cabinets before pulling out half a loaf of bread and peanut butter. She made sandwiches while Grant sipped the bourbon.

As she handed him a sandwich, he confessed. "I'm scaring myself, to be honest." While they ate, he filled her in on what he learned at the Hack-A-Thon Friday morning.

Darlene's eyes widened, sandwich frozen in midair. "A nuclear attack? Are you sure?"

"No, but better safe than sorry. He finished his drink

and set the glass on the table. "First thing tomorrow, you should get food, water, and as many supplies as you can think of. If what I learned is true, it could happen anytime."

"Will Charlotte be hit?"

Grant nodded. "It's one of the top twenty-five, isn't it?"

"I think so."

"Should we leave? Go into the country?"

Grant shrugged. "Do you have somewhere you can go?"

"No."

"Then stay here. As long as you get in the basement, you should be okay. You're pretty far from downtown."

Darlene drained the rest of her glass and collected the now-empty plates. "We should get some sleep. I'll grab you a blanket and some pillows. You can sleep on the couch."

She walked out of the room and Grant stared at the space she left. He didn't know what to make of her abrupt departure. Denial? Fear? He scrubbed a hand down his face and let a yawn distort his features.

Whatever it was, Darlene was right. He needed some sleep.

He stood and made his way down a short hall to a living room.

Darlene held out a folded blanket and a pillow. "Sorry I don't have a guest room."

"That's all right." He took the bedding with a smile. "Thank you for letting me stay."

She nodded. "No problem. Good night." She left before Grant could say another word.

He eased down to the couch and slid off his shoes. After a few hours of sleep, he would hit the road. He pulled out his phone and turned it on.

One voicemail and missed call.

He swiped it open and hit play.

CHAPTER TEN

LEAH

Georgia Memorial Hospital
   Downtown Atlanta
   Saturday, 7:00 a.m.

Leah woke up to pain radiating down her neck. Sleeping curled up in a ball in a threadbare chair might not have been the best strategy. She rubbed the knot in her muscle and sat up.

The breakroom could have been a refugee camp. Nurses and doctors slept in every available chair, using their lab coats or extra hospital sheets as blankets.

Leah stood up, wincing as her legs ached in protest. After fishing out a backup pair of scrubs from her locker, she cleaned up and changed in the bathroom.

With a tight ponytail, clean face, and new clothes, she almost felt human. Tiptoeing around the sleeping bodies, she searched for Dr. Phillips. He wasn't there.

Guess she would be heading out alone. Leah packed her things as quietly as possible and slung her duffel across her body.

It would be a long trek to her sister's place in Hampton, but Leah would get there. She promised Grant.

As she walked toward the hall, a shadow fell across the doorway. Dr. Phillips. Leah almost didn't recognize him in street clothes. With running shoes, jeans, and a sweatshirt, he looked a decade younger. She smiled and walked over.

"Are you ready?"

She nodded.

"Then we should go."

Together, they walked toward the employee entrance on the east side of the first floor.

"You sure about leaving?"

Dr. Phillips glanced at Leah. "Of course. Aren't you?"

Leah hesitated. "They could use our help."

"I'm sure that's true. But I've pulled a forty-eight-hour shift and you worked twenty at least. We need to go home to our families. They need us, too."

Leah turned to look behind her. The hospital had quieted overnight. Without the usual influx of ambulances and EMTs, the ER was almost peaceful. "I guess you're right."

Dr. Phillips opened the door and Leah stepped out onto the sidewalk. She stopped and tapped her head. "I forgot my car's in the deck. I should check to see if it starts."

"It won't." Dr. Phillips took off walking down the sidewalk and after a moment, Leah caught up. "I've been awake for a while. I talked to the staff. No one's vehicles work. I tried mine; no luck."

"But someone said older cars still functioned." Leah tried to remember who it was and more of the conversation, but it was all a blur. Exhaustion always wrecked her memory.

Dr. Phillips shrugged. "Maybe we'll get lucky and find one. Until then, we're walking."

Leah cast a sideways glance at the doctor as they walked. Without his lab coat, she could see he kept in shape. Strong legs, capable arms. The wrinkles around his eyes and the highlights in his brown hair spoke of time in the sun. "So where do you live?"

"On the north side of town, just past the malls. You?"

"Outside the perimeter. But I'm heading to my sister's place in Hampton."

Dr. Phillips whistled. "That's forty miles."

"I know."

"We'll need to find a car."

"Dr Phillips, I don't—"

He stopped walking. "Andy. Call me Andy."

Leah opened her mouth, but turned the shock into a smile. "Leah."

"Nice you meet you, Leah." The doctor stuck out his hand and she shook it with a laugh.

"Now what's this about not finding a car?"

She tucked a strand of hair behind her ear and resumed walking. "I don't know if I'm ready to start stealing."

Andy nodded. "Fair enough." They walked to the corner and glanced both ways before crossing the street. Eight in the morning on a Saturday, downtown was ordinarily a ghost town. Today, cars littered the street, stalled out from the EMP the night before.

People slept in their back seats, still wearing suits from their fancy jobs in the high-rises all above them. One woman sat in the driver's seat of a BMW, pushing the start button over and over.

Leah and Andy avoided her as they snaked through the tangled mess. They turned the corner and headed north toward midtown.

"So tell me about you."

Leah snorted. "Me? I'm boring."

"Nonsense. There's got to be something."

Leah ran through the basics. "I've worked at Georgia Memorial for three years. I'm married, no kids. Live just outside the city in a cookie-cutter subdivision." She shrugged. "See? Dull as a doornail."

Andy gave her a nudge. "Come on. Think bigger. What do you do for fun?"

She smacked her lips. "Read?"

"There we go. What types of books? You strike me as the thriller sort."

"You'll laugh."

He fixed the doctor look on her, the one that gets

patients to tell them everything. She blurted it out. "Romance novels."

Andy laughed. "And here I thought you'd say something like self-help."

Leah rolled her eyes. "Your turn."

He held up a fist, sticking out a finger for every point. "Married. Live about five miles due north in an overpriced house in a good school district. Two fur kids, but we're trying for the real deal. My wife's name is Marley but if you call her that, she'll shiv you."

Leah laughed. "I like your wife already."

"Everyone does." His tone turned somber. "I need to get home."

"I know."

They lapsed into silence and picked up the pace, making it out of downtown and into midtown within the hour.

As they crossed another congested street, Leah's stomach growled.

"Is that you or a bear cub in your duffel?"

"Me, I'm afraid. I haven't eaten in a while."

Andy surveyed the street. "Let's change that." He pointed at a restaurant with an open front door a hundred feet ahead.

They slipped inside.

Leah squinted and blinked, her eyes working overtime to adjust to the dim light.

A burly man with a grease-stained apron approached from the back. "Can I help you?"

"Are you open?"

He nodded. "Cash only, limited service."

Andy spoke up. "Works for us."

Together they followed the man to the last empty table by the window. He cleared his throat. "I've got sandwiches. Ham, turkey, roast beef. White or wheat."

"Any breakfast?"

He stared at Leah like she'd turned him to stone. "I said limited service. Take it or leave it."

Andy reached into his back pocket. "How much for a sandwich?"

"Ten dollars. Chips are two dollars extra."

Leah grimaced at the prices. "Does that include cheese?"

The man pinned her with the same look.

"Guess not." She rummaged through her bag and pulled out her wallet before counting her cash. She almost never carried any now that everywhere took cards. "I've only got seven."

Andy waved her off. "I've got enough."

"You sure?"

He nodded and turned to the man. "I'll take a ham on wheat and whatever chips you have."

Leah swallowed. "Turkey on white, please."

"Chips?"

She glanced at Andy and he encouraged her. "Yes, please."

"Twenty-four dollars. Pay in advance."

The man waited while Andy counted up his money and placed it in his meaty palm. Then he turned without a word and walked away.

"Not big on customer service, is he?"

"I'm guessing he spends most of his time in the kitchen." Leah pulled her coat closer and looked around the restaurant. Three other tables held customers. A pair of twenty-somethings in pajamas, an older woman alone, and a pair of police officers.

Leah motioned at the cops. "Think they know anything?"

Andy turned around to look. "More than we do, probably."

She ached to get up and ask them if they knew what caused the blackout, and if what the guy from the phone company said were true. Her mind tripped over all the messages Grant left her while she was busy rocking preemies in the NICU and helping trauma patients in the ER.

Her husband insisted she get out of the city as fast as she could, claiming she wasn't safe and more things were going to happen. She wished he'd been clearer and explained what he knew. She didn't understand why he was speaking in generalities.

Was he in trouble? Were people listening? Fear iced down her spine. If something happened to Grant, how would she carry on? Leah jumped when two glasses of water *thunked* onto the table.

The man who took her order pointed at them both. "No ice."

He stomped off and Leah took a chance. "I'll be right back."

Before Andy could say anything, she walked over to

the police officers and plastered on her most helpful, nonconfrontational smile. "Hi."

They eyed her with suspicion. The male officer inclined his head. "Hello."

"I'm sorry to bother you, but do you know anything about what happened last night? The power is still off and my car doesn't work and—"

The cop held up his hand. "All we know is that it's widespread. Whatever knocked the power out did so up and down the East Coast."

Leah swallowed. That part was true. "No one's said anything about what it could be?"

The police shared a glance. "Nothing definite."

"Any word on when we'll find out?"

He shook his head. "Sorry."

Leah smiled and thanked them before heading back to the table. A turkey sandwich sat at her place along with a snack-size bag of Fritos. She held up the little bag. "Two dollars for this?"

Andy shrugged as he took a bite of sandwich. "Guess price gouging's already a thing."

Leah took a bite of her own sandwich and sighed. "At least it's good."

She chomped down on her sandwich as Andy attacked his own. They cleared their plates and polished off their chips in record time.

"You think he's got any dessert?"

"For twenty bucks, he'll probably give you a lollipop."

Andy laughed, but the sound was cut off by a massive rumble. The windows rattled, the table shook, and Leah jumped to her feet. The front of the building across the street burst apart in a terrific explosion. Bits of brick and glass flew into the road and Leah ducked for cover.

Andy scrambled to join her beneath the table. "What the hell?"

She shook her head. "I don't know. An explosion?" She risked a glance above the table top. A giant gaping maw of brick and broken glass belched flames and smoke in the building across the street. Whatever happened, it was contained to one small area. it wasn't the end of the world.

Leah sucked in a breath and stood up as the police officers sprang into action. The female officer keyed the radio on her shoulder and spoke into it. "One Adam fourteen, I have a code thirty-three at the intersection of Sage and Fourteenth."

The radio crackled. "Copy one Adam fourteen, sending any available units to your location."

The officer pulled her service weapon from its holster. Leah watched as both officers slipped from the restaurant and disappeared from view. She turned to Andy. "Do you know what that means?"

He grabbed his bag. "No. And I don't want to stay to find out."

CHAPTER ELEVEN

GRANT

Suburbs of Charlotte, North Carolina
Saturday, 8:00 a.m.

Grant stretched and his arm hit a lamp shade behind him. He reached out and caught the base before the lamp crashed to the floor and woke the whole house. As he turned to sit up, a pair of little bare feet caught his eye.

"Hello."

A boy of seven or eight stood in front of the couch wearing red and blue striped pajamas and a serious case of bed head. The kid tilted his head just like his mother. "Who are you?"

Grant wiped the sleep from his eyes and smiled. "A friend of your mother's."

"What are you doing here?"

"I needed a place to sleep."

"Don't you have a home?"

Grant held back a laugh. Darlene's son didn't hesitate to ask what was on his mind. "I live in Atlanta. It's a long way away."

The boy turned around without another word and padded into the kitchen. Grant watched him go before finding the bathroom down the hall. He splashed water on his face and took stock. Bags hung under his eyes. His hair stuck up in all directions. His clothes were rumpled.

I look like a bum.

He exhaled and replayed Leah's voicemail from the night before. She was still downtown helping at the hospital. Grant clutched the sink as nausea roiled his stomach.

He didn't know if he should laugh, cry, or scream. Was he really putting his trust in a teenage kid who broke into third-party software on the web but couldn't tie his shoes? Baker, the hacker who discovered the threat, wasn't the most reliable source. If Grant were a police officer, he'd probably laugh the kid out of the building.

But Midge took it seriously. Yeah, she was a hacker just like Baker, but she discounted him, too. It was only when she read the underlying documentation that she spooked. Grant pushed off the sink and clenched his fists. He had to assume it was real. He already told his boss to stuff it, left the conference, and stole a car. What choice did he have but to carry on?

Grant reached into his pocket and pulled out his phone. He clicked it on and opened up the photos. His wife's beautiful face stared out at him, blue eyes sparkling, hair like spun sunshine. If she stayed at the hospital and the bombs hit, surely she would die.

Damn it. He should have told her everything he knew. Screw the potential panic or someone listening. He should have shouted from the rooftops about the nuclear threat and to get the hell out of the cities. Instead, he fumbled around like an idiot, telling her only that it was dangerous and she needed to be safe.

I failed her, and for what? To not scare her?

With the palms of his hands, he pressed on his shut eyes until they hurt. If Leah died it would be his fault. He brought his hands down and stared at himself again in the mirror. Was he really giving up now? Was he going to stand there and curse himself and call it hopeless?

Grant squared his shoulders. *No. I won't let that happen. I will find a way to get to her. Leah won't face the end alone.*

With a ragged exhale, Grant left the bathroom and made his way to the kitchen. The boy stood on a stool pouring cereal into a plastic bowl, the picture of normal, everyday life. Grant forced his panic down. Matthew and Darlene needed help, too. He told Darlene the basics last night, but what about Matthew? He couldn't grab his bag and run without at least testing the kid's resolve. Leah would never forgive him.

The boy struggled with the plastic sleeve in the box and Grant opened his mouth to offer help, but caught himself without saying a word. He remembered fiercely clinging to independence as a kid. When a grownup cut in, he always took it as an insult. Instead, he closed his mouth and leaned against the door frame, waiting.

At last the boy finished closing the box and picked up the milk. As he poured it on his cereal, Grant eased into the room. "It's Matthew, right?"

The kid nodded before carrying his bowl to the table.

"My name's Grant."

Matthew slurped a spoonful of Cheerios into his mouth.

"How's your mom these days?"

Matthew swallowed the bite. "She tries."

Grant blinked.

"But she's tired all the time. She works too hard and worries too much."

"It's just you and her?"

Matthew nodded before chomping down another spoonful.

Grant hesitated. The kid seemed more levelheaded than his mother, but he was young. Could he handle what might be coming?

The kid broke the silence. "Something bad happened, didn't it?"

"How do you know?"

"Liv freaked out last night. When the lights went out, she couldn't text anyone or get online. She said it was the end of the world."

"Because the internet was down?"

Matthew nodded.

Grant supposed a teenager would think that. Typing to friends and taking pictures to post online was the new pastime. No one under the age of twenty talked or hung out anymore. They just sat with their necks bent, furiously pecking at their phones like a row of birds.

He hedged. "It's not the end of the world, but something worse is coming." Grant leaned an arm on the table. "Do you know what a bomb is?"

"Something that explodes. Hurts a lot of people."

Grant nodded. "A bomb might go off here, in Charlotte. A big one. If that happens, you'll need to go in the basement and hide. Can you do that?"

"Will my mom have to hide, too?"

"Yes. Everyone will. For a few days until it's safe to go out."

"Okay." Matthew took another bite. "After that, will everything be back to normal?"

"No." Grant focused on the table and the grains of the dark wood. "Nothing will ever be back to normal again."

"Good."

Grant flicked his eyes up to meet Mathew's solid stare. "Why?"

"Because normal isn't all that great."

"It'll be hard."

"I know."

Grant marveled at the little guy. If anyone could make it through what happened next, Matthew could. He pushed up to stand. "Will you be all right?"

Matthew nodded.

"I'm going to clean up and head out. Tell your mom thanks for the couch." He walked back to the living room and opened his suitcase. He pulled out the workout gear he never had a chance to use at the conference and his toiletry kit, and returned to the hall bath.

A half an hour later, Grant emerged clean and ready. He packed his suitcase with everything except a bottle of Gatorade and a granola bar and walked to the door. Matthew stood in the archway to the kitchen, watching.

"Remember what I said. Get in the basement and stay there."

"I will."

Grant nodded at him and walked outside. The cold morning air bit into his sweatshirt and he hustled to the car. He tossed the suitcase into the back seat before sliding into the driver's seat. The front curtain fluttered as he tapped the two starter wires together.

As he sat back up, Darlene rushed from the house. Grant rolled down the window.

"You're leaving."

He nodded. "I need to find Leah."

Darlene pulled a bathrobe tight around her middle. Without makeup and her hair pulled back in a ponytail, she seemed so small and vulnerable. Grant swallowed. He couldn't stay even if she needed him to.

She stuck out a hand. In it, the hundred dollar bill he'd given her the day before flapped in the wind. "Take it."

"No. I paid you that fair and square."

"But the car didn't work and you probably saved my life. Matthew's, too. Take it." She shoved it at him again.

Grant took the money. "Thanks."

"I hope you find your wife."

"Me, too." He glanced up at the window. Matthew stood between the curtain and the glass, watching. "When the bomb hits—"

"Go to the basement. I know."

Grant flashed a tight smile and put the car in reverse. Darlene stepped back and he backed out of her driveway. He glanced at the fuel gauge as he put it in drive. *First stop: gas.*

CHAPTER TWELVE

LEAH

Midtown Atlanta
    Saturday, 10:00 a.m.

Flames leapt from the shattered window across the street and Leah grabbed Andy's arm. "We can't leave. There could be survivors."

"So?"

"We need to help them."

"Are you crazy?"

"No. I'm a nurse. And you're a doctor."

"I'm not a miracle worker. You see the size of those flames? Whoever's in there is a human barbecue at this point."

Leah's eyes bugged. "Are you telling me that you're willing to turn your back on injured people because they might not survive?"

Andy ran a hand through his hair. "I'm making an educated guess and reminding you we need to get home. Stopping to help doesn't accomplish that."

"But it's the right thing to do."

"No, it's not." Andy slung his bag over his shoulder and walked out of the restaurant.

Leah followed. She palmed her hips. "Do you want me to tell that stingy guy in the restaurant that you stole an extra bag of chips?"

Andy spun around. "You wouldn't!"

Leah fixed him with a stare and Andy threw up his hands. "You're as bad as my wife."

"I'll take that as a compliment."

"Don't." Andy turned toward the source of the explosion with a snort. "If this goes to hell, I'm blaming you."

Leah nodded and hustled to join Andy as he crossed the street.

The female police officer held up her hand. "Stay back!"

Leah stuck her hospital ID in the air. "We're from Georgia Memorial. I'm an RN and he's a doctor. We can help."

The cop eyed Leah's ID and asked for Andy's as well. After inspecting them for a moment, she nodded. "All right. But you follow orders. I can't have more injuries on my hands."

"Coming out with a bleeder!" The male cop clambered out of the door to the building and smoke billowed in his wake. He set a man with burn marks tracking down his left side on the ground.

As soon as the cop stood up, he doubled back over and coughed. Andy rushed up to him. "I'm a doctor. You need to take slow, measured breaths. That will calm your lungs and open your airway."

The cop nodded.

Leah crouched beside the burned man. The burns were worse than she feared. His shirt was melted to his skin in several places and his thigh was seared to the bone. The camouflage pattern of his pants matched the pattern of the burn. It was gruesome and Leah struggled not to be sick.

He would never survive.

She forced herself to smile. "Hi, I'm Leah and I'll be taking care of you."

The man reached up with his non-burned hand, scrabbling for her arm.

"Can you tell me what happened, sir?"

His eyes glazed over and spit dribbled from his chin.

Andy kneeled beside him. He jerked back when got a look at the injuries.

"How's the cop?"

"He'll live." Andy glanced up at Leah. The meaning of his words was plain.

Leah nodded. She knew the man lying on the sidewalk was a goner. She only wanted to make him comfortable for his final moments. She smiled at him again. "Sir? Can you hear me?"

The man's mouth worked open and shut.

"He's gone, Leah."

"No, he's not." She leaned closer. "Sir, is there someone you want me to contact? Some family member?"

The man moaned. "Bombs!"

Leah frowned. "Sir? I can't understand you."

He focused on Leah, his pupils contracting as he brought her into focus. "You need to save yourself."

"From what?"

"The bombs. They're coming!"

She glanced up at the cops. They were talking into their radios and not paying any attention. She turned back to the victim. "I don't understand. What bombs? You mean the blackout?"

"No! That was just the beginning. A first strike intended to hamper our defenses." He reached up again and found her arm. His fingers gripped it tight. "The real attack is coming."

Leah swallowed. "What attack? What is it?"

His voice grew quiet. "Nuclear bombs."

"How do you know? Where did you hear this? Sir?"

"Get out." He coughed and blood dribbled down his chin. "Get out before it's too late." His hand slipped from Leah's arm and she felt the non-charred portion of his neck for a pulse. He was gone.

Leah leaned back on her heels and looked up as the male police officer stepped over.

"Did he tell you anything?"

Leah stood up. "He said we were under attack. That the blackout was just the beginning."

"What did he say was next?"

"A nuclear bomb."

The cop snorted. "Yeah, right. And I'm the president's uncle." He pointed at the building. "Idiot was trying to rig up a generator in an enclosed room. A bunker-type thing made of concrete block. Blew himself up instead."

Leah stared at the man's body. "I'm sorry we couldn't save him."

"It's okay. You did the best you could."

The cop stepped away and Andy pulled Leah to the side. "Are you crazy? Why are you telling the cop about that man's delusions?"

"He asked."

"Next time, don't say a word unless you want to get stuck at a crime scene for hours."

Leah yanked her arm away. "What are you talking about?"

"Any time you tell a cop anything, they have to file a report. If you're a witness, it can take forever. Never, ever tell them anything. Never make yourself a target."

"I'm not a target. I'm a nurse and that man needed help. I only told the truth."

"Sometimes the truth is all it takes to turn a good day into the worst day of your life."

Leah stared at Andy as he stalked over to his bag and slung it over his shoulder. Had he lost his mind? She picked up her bag and walked over to the police officers. "I'm sorry we couldn't be of more help. Do you need us to stay?"

The male cop shook his head. "Naw. You go on. We'll handle it."

Leah smiled and hurried over to Andy. "See? We didn't have to stay."

"Lucky us." He pulled his pack of cigarettes from his bag and shook it, muttering beneath his breath.

"Do you really think those were delusions?"

He fished a cigarette from the pack and tapped it on his palm before putting it in his mouth. "Of course. Don't you?"

Leah waited for Andy to light the cigarette and stash the almost-empty pack and lighter before she responded. "The more I think about it, the more I think it might be true."

He took a drag and puffed the smoke into the air. "Did you hit your head yesterday?"

"No." Leah scowled. "But between my husband's messages, what the cell phone guy said, and now the burn victim, it's all adding up."

"It's a blackout. A really big blackout."

"What about the man in the hospital who claimed it was a high-altitude nuclear weapon? What if that was only what the dead guy called it... A first strike?"

"Nonsense. Who would go to all the trouble to blackout half the United States only to drop a bomb on us a few hours later?"

Andy had a point. Maybe it was overkill. Maybe she was reading too much into everything because Grant wasn't there and she couldn't reach him. Leah pulled out her phone and tried to call. She screamed when the busy signal sounded in her ear.

"Guess you aren't lucky after all."

Leah exhaled and shoved the phone back in her pocket. "What do you know about nuclear bombs?"

"Not much. We learned how to respond back in med school."

"Tell me."

Andy sucked down some more smoke and nicotine and exhaled. "If you're in the blast radius, forget it, you're incinerated. The bombs are super strong and they displace a ton of energy, so buildings will be blown apart at the site of the explosion."

"What about farther out?"

"How big a bomb are we talking about?"

Leah shook her head. "How about what was dropped on Japan?"

"In World War II?"

She nodded.

"Then once you're outside the immediate vicinity, there's a fifty-fifty chance of survival for about a two-mile radius. Think the biggest hurricane you've ever seen blasting scorching-hot wind in every direction."

Andy paused to smoke. "If a building doesn't fall on you and you're not outside and burned to a crisp when it explodes, you might live through the initial blast. Beyond the first two miles, you would survive, maybe have some injuries from debris. But that's not the worst."

"It's not?"

Andy finished his cigarette and put it out in the gutter. "No. As early as twenty or thirty minutes, all the radiation released into the atmosphere will start falling back to earth."

"Radiation sickness."

"Exactly. If you don't get underground or in a secure building that's completely closed to the outside, you'll be exposed to enough radiation to kill you. It might take days or weeks, but eventually, you'll succumb to the sickness."

Leah blew out a breath. "How long does the radiation last?"

"Not as long as you think. Within two weeks, it would be practically gone."

Leah gave a start. "Everyone has to shelter in place for two weeks?"

"That's for the radiation to be virtually eliminated. After seventy hours, with the right gear, you could go outside."

"A hazmat suit."

"At a minimum."

Leah ran a hand over her head. It couldn't be real. But what if? She thought about her husband's messages begging her to get out of the city and go to her sister's place. Hampton was forty miles from the hospital.

There would be no radiation there. She would be safe.

Leah stopped in the middle of the sidewalk. Did Grant know? Did he know about the bombs and try to warn her?

Andy stopped a few paces ahead. And cocked his head. "Do you hear that?"

Leah rushed forward. "What?"

He held up a hand to shush her and strained to listen.

The faintest sound of someone talking found Leah's ear.

Andy nodded. "I know that sound anywhere. It's a television. Someone's watching *Seinfeld*."

CHAPTER THIRTEEN

GRANT

Suburbs of Charlotte, North Carolina
Saturday, 10:30 a.m.

It took Grant an hour to find an open gas station. Every one he drove past was either dark and closed up or sported a makeshift sign stating *Closed Until Further Notice*.

He eased the Cutlass up to a pump and killed the engine. The car clinked and groaned as it cooled and Grant listened, waiting. The downside to not having keys was the lack of security. He couldn't lock the car and anyone with half a brain could touch the starter wires together and rev it up.

When it appeared no one would come outside to check on him, Grant exited the vehicle. He hoped the hundred dollars Darlene returned would be enough. The

Cutlass guzzled gas like a parched man drank water. It was always thirsty.

He walked toward the gas station's convenience store with his hands in his pockets and his wife on his mind. Was she still at the hospital? Would he make it home in time? It wasn't until he reached for the door handle that Grant heard the shouts.

Flattening his body against the wall, he sucked in a breath and listened.

"Gimme the money, man!"

A low voice responded and Grant couldn't make out the words.

"Do it! Or I'll drop you!"

Grant swallowed. He showed up in time for a robbery. *Just my luck.* He ran a hand down his face as the same low voice responded.

The military man inside Grant ached to join the tussle, but it had been years since he served and he wasn't armed. He scanned the area for a weapon. The outside of the gas station sported an ice machine with water leaking from the corner, a stack of firewood for sale, and an air machine. Nothing helpful.

"I'm not playin'! Give it to me!"

If the man offering the threats had a gun, Grant couldn't disarm him easily. If the guy was quick with the trigger finger, all bets were off. *Hell.*

He couldn't turn around and leave. Filling his tank was too important. Grant needed gas.

The robber's voice edged up a notch as he yelled a

string of obscenities. Frustration could be good; it meant he either wasn't armed or didn't want to shoot.

Grant's gaze settled on the ice machine. Distraction would be key. He stripped out of his sweatshirt and hustled over to the leaking machine. As fast as possible, he scooped up the melted ice water and dumped it down the front of his shirt and into his hair.

The cold shocked him, but he jumped to get the blood flowing and smacked his cheeks a few times. Adrenaline did the rest.

He shook himself off and yanked open the door. "Man, it's hot for January. Hey, you got some cold Gatorade up in this joint?"

A single man with a shotgun spun around and pointed it at Grant. He couldn't have been older than twenty, with a half-grown goatee and a sparkly earring in his ear. From the way he held the gun at his waist and not tight to his shoulder, Grant knew the kid didn't have a clue how to shoot it.

Thank God for small favors. Grant held up his hands. "Whoa, easy there." He scanned the room as he begged off. "I just need to rehydrate before I dehydrate, know what I mean?" He staggered a few steps into the store and paused by a display of golf umbrellas. *Those will do.*

"Stop or I'll shoot!" The gunman waved the shotgun at Grant and scowled.

"Naw, man you don't wanna shoot me. I'm just in need of electrolytes." Grant bobbed in front of the umbrella stand and wiped his wet forehead with his sleeve. He made eye contact with the clerk, an older man of about fifty with a stern face and thick neck.

"Sports drinks are on the back wall."

Grant grinned like he'd won the lottery. He pointed his fingers in the shape of a gun at the clerk while he pulled an umbrella from the stand with his free hand. It hung loose in his fingers. *Solid handle. Metal shaft. Good choice.*

He spun around. "Now there is a man who knows his store. Can't get service like that just anywhere."

The gunman stood frozen, still pointing his gun at Grant, but not knowing what to do. It was rule number one: always be unpredictable. Inexperienced attackers expected people to stand still or drop to the ground, not act a fool and cause a scene.

It wouldn't work with a seasoned guy who knew his way around a crime, but Grant was lucky. He'd thrown the kid off-balance. He fluffed his shirt and dropped his knee in a fake swagger as he walked by, but it was all a ploy. As he bent down, he swung the umbrella. A hard, quick chop to the gunman's left knee and he buckled.

With the shotgun at the kid's waist and pain radiating up his leg, he didn't have the strength required to pull the trigger. The kid struggled with the gun as he hopped on his good leg. Grant grabbed the barrel with his left hand and wrenched it free.

Whipping around, Grant checked to confirm the gun was loaded, and brought the butt tight to his shoulder. He pointed it at the kid now clutching his busted knee.

Grant directed his words at the clerk, all pretense and fake swagger gone. "What do you want to do with him?"

The clerk came out from around the counter, a shotgun of his own in his hands. "Kick him out." He grabbed the guy by the scruff of the neck. "If you ever come in here again, I'll shoot first." He threw him out of the store and pulled the door shut before locking it.

"Damn kids. The power goes out and they think they own the place." The clerk moved his shotgun to his left hand and stuck out a meaty paw. "Billy Orson, owner and manager. Nice to meet you."

Grant shook the man's hand. "Grant Walton. Same here. Sorry if I interrupted your plans." He pointed at the clerk's gun. "Looks like you had it under control."

"No worries. I'm glad you took out his knee. Then I didn't have to mop up his blood."

Grant raised his eyebrows as Billy walked back around the counter. He was pretty sure the man meant every word.

"So what can I do for you, Mr. Walton?"

Grant smoothed back his hair. "I've got a gas guzzler and I'm running on fumes. I'm hoping I can fill up."

Billy nodded, impressed. "You've got a working car?"

"A '77 Cutlass Supreme."

Billy's face contorted into a grin. "You don't say! Mind if I take a look?"

Grant held out his hand. "Be my guest." He grabbed his sweatshirt where he dropped it by the front door and followed Billy to the car.

The bigger man laughed and it shook his belly. "I

haven't seen one of these since I was a teenager. Used to tinker with my friend's on the weekends." He bent to check out the wheels. "It's even got the spokes!"

Grant smiled. A man after his own heart. Chatting with Billy about the past would be a good way to spend an afternoon. Too bad he couldn't stay. "About that gas."

Billy nodded. "I've got a generator. It'll take a minute to get running, but I can do it."

"How much to fill her up?"

Billy closed one eye as he thought it over. "For you, free of charge."

Grant waved him off. "I'll pay for it."

"I don't think I'll have a lot of customers eager for gas today. It's free, I mean it. But if you want to buy some food or drinks, that'll cost you."

Grant thought it over and nodded. "Fair enough." As the owner headed back inside the store, Grant waited by the Cutlass. A few minutes later, he heard a generator gurgle and roar to life. The hum of the motor drowned out everything else. He wouldn't be able to hear a car, a band of thugs, or anything.

He checked the shotgun over, confirming it was operational and surveyed the street. The sound of a generator could attract a crowd.

A minute later, Billy huffed over and motioned for Grant to open the gas cover on the Cutlass. He did and waited as Billy turned the pump on and used his key to override the payment option. Grant pumped a full tank of gas and Billy reversed the process, shutting down the pump before turning off the generator.

The silence hit Grant like a slap. He hurried back inside the store and grabbed a bottle of warm Gatorade, a stack of Power Bars, and a map of North Carolina. He set it all on the counter.

Billy rang him up. "Fourteen eighty-two."

Grant handed over his twenty and Billy handed him the change. "Thanks."

"Thank you. If you're ever back in Charlotte and you need to fill that beauty up, just swing on by. I'll take care of you."

Grant nodded and walked out the door. He checked his watch. *Eleven thirty already.* He hurried to the Cutlass and started it up. Even if he could get up to highway speeds, a full tank would only get him two hundred miles, maybe a bit more.

Grant pulled out the map. Taking I-85 would get him to the hospital in two hundred and fifty miles give or take, but he'd never be able to navigate it. With all the cars stalled out on the highway, he'd be lucky to make it a mile.

Back roads would be even longer. Grant frowned. He'd have to find gas and another map somewhere in South Carolina. He put the car in drive and eased onto the road. He'd be lucky if he reached the Atlanta city limits before dark.

CHAPTER FOURTEEN

LEAH

Midtown Atlanta
Saturday, 1:00 p.m.

Leah followed Andy as he searched for the source of the noise. She couldn't shake the words of the dying man loose from her head. "The more I think about it, the more I think he's right."

"Who?" Andy stopped in the middle of the sidewalk to listen before altering course.

"The fire bug."

"You must be suffering from smoke inhalation."

Leah cut him a glance. "That's you with all those cigarettes you've been smoking."

Andy smirked. "If it's the end of the world like you say, then what does it matter?"

"What he said makes sense."

"No, it doesn't." Andy held up his hand. "Hush! I

hear it again." He closed his eyes and listened. "It's that way." He took off toward the east, darting down a side street with his head tilted toward the noise.

Leah rushed to follow. "Why are you even searching for whatever it is? We need to be headed north."

Andy waved her off. "If there's a TV, that means someone has power. We can check the news, maybe make a call."

"It's probably some guy with a generator like the one that just blew up. We don't even know if any news channels are broadcasting."

"Someone is, somewhere. They have to be." Andy kept hunting, stopping every ten steps to listen. As they approached the park, more and more people appeared. Some walked dogs, others stood in little groups, chatting and shaking heads. On the stoop of the closest building, four or five people sat with beers in their hands and confusion on their faces.

It was a cold day to be standing around outside, but what else could they do? Without power or working cars or calls going through, talking was all people had left.

Cars clogged the main street up ahead and Leah's frown deepened. She hurried to catch up to Andy. "We're wasting time."

"No, we're not." He pointed with a grin. "There it is! See!" His finger jabbed up toward the second story of an old apartment building at the intersection of the side street they had walked down and the clogged street fronting the park. Through the window, Leah could make out a faint blue glow.

While she stayed on the sidewalk, Andy scurried into the alley between the building and the one beside it, darting around potholes and a dumpster to stop below the iron balcony.

He cupped his hands and shouted toward the open window. "Hello!"

Leah rushed forward. "You shouldn't be shouting!"

"Why not? I want to watch that TV." He tried again. "Hey, guy up there!" Andy spun around beneath the window before grabbing the balcony post and giving it a shake.

"What are you doing?"

"Trying to find a way up."

"Have you lost your mind?" Leah grabbed his arm. "We need to go. Someone's going to come down here and ask what's going on. Come on." She yanked harder, but Andy shoved her off.

"Hey, guy with the TV!"

A head poked out the window. "What the hell is it?"

"Is that a TV you've got running?"

"What's it to you?"

"Can you get the news?"

The guy glanced back inside. "Maybe."

Andy reached into his pocket and pulled out a ten dollar bill. "Ten dollars for ten minutes."

"Five minutes."

"Seven."

"Deal. Unit 201."

Andy's face glowed. Leah fought the urge to throw up.

She followed Andy back to the front of the building
with unease percolating in her gut. They eased through
the antique gate separating the building's courtyard from
the street and walked up to the front door. Someone had
propped it open with a brick.

"Guess I should have tried this first." Andy shrugged
and pulled the door open before ushering Leah inside.

She stood on the faded lavender carpet and looked
around. The building had seen better days. Paint peeled
off the trim. Dirt and grime coated the brass mailboxes,
turning them brown. Foot traffic had worn a threadbare
strip down the center of the stairs.

Andy didn't seem to notice. He took the stairs two at
a time and bopped up and down at the top, barely able to
wait for Leah to catch up. He banged on Unit 201's door.

It unlocked and a grizzled old man approaching
eighty stuck out a shriveled hand. "Ten bucks."

Andy deposited the money in the man's palm and he
stepped back. The smell of dust and old man hit Leah
and she brought her sleeve up to her face.

"It's crowded. Watch your step." The man turned
around and left the two of them standing in his
open door.

They eased inside and Andy shut it behind him.
Crowded was an understatement. Stacks of newspapers
lined the narrow hall, some taller than Leah herself.
They scooted by single file, passing a kitchen that Leah
refused to look at. The smell alone would give her
nightmares.

Andy stopped on the threshold to the living room and

Leah squeaked by to stand beside him. *Oh, my.* The man took hoarding to a whole new level. Every surface was full of... stuff.

What must have been the dining room table was covered with three feet of magazines. All along the wall cardboard boxes overflowed with everything from baseball mitts to broken lamps to a... *Is that a cat carrier?*

Leah shook her head. One glimpse of an emaciated cat and she was leaving. She focused on the old man. "You live here?"

"You got a problem with that?"

"It's a little messy."

"Maid quit." The man fumbled with a rabbit-ear antenna attached to an ancient tube TV.

Andy stepped into the room, avoiding the largest piles of debris. "How are you running that?"

The man snorted like it was obvious. "Marine battery and a 400-watt inverter."

Leah drummed her fingers on her arm as she waited for the old man to change the channel. Pixels distorted the picture. Leah squinted.

A reporter stood outside what looked like a Spanish-style mansion. The man fiddled some more. The picture came in along with the sound.

"Like I said earlier, Chip, we're on hour twenty of the largest blackout in history. The entire eastern half of the United States is without power."

Leah shuddered.

A man's voice answered on the TV. "For those just

tuning in, we're speaking with our reporter on the street, Lainey Sinclair. Where are you, Lainey?"

"I'm standing outside the British Consulate-General here in Los Angeles. According to British intelligence, there is credible evidence that the blackout was caused by a nuclear weapon."

"Do they know any details?"

"According to my sources, they claim a high-altitude missile carrying a nuclear bomb detonated at two o'clock Pacific Standard Time yesterday somewhere above Washington, DC."

"What does that mean?"

"The bomb set off what's called an electromagnetic pulse, or EMP, that has knocked out power across the eastern half of the United States, from Ohio to the coast and from New York City all the way to Orlando. We're getting reports that Miami and portions of upstate New York and into New Hampshire, Vermont, and Maine are online and fully operational."

"When will the power be restored?"

"We don't know, Chip."

The man's voice boomed out of the speakers. "You've heard it folks. British intelligence is confirming what our sources on the ground have seen. Combine the grid failure with what appears to be a mass disruption to late-model cars, and we've got a disaster on our hands."

Leah sucked in a breath and wrapped her arms around her middle. It was as bad as she feared. Andy stood beside her, frozen to the spot, his mouth working back and forth as he processed the reporter's news.

It wasn't just a blackout. It was a terrorist attack or an act of war. Why wasn't the news station talking about who was responsible? Where was the United States government in all of this?

The woman on TV appeared exhausted, with blonde hair pulled back off her face with a headband and a dress that held more wrinkles than Leah's scrubs. Had she been reporting since the power went out?

She cleared her throat and stepped closer to the camera. "What's more important, Chip, are the latest reports from intelligence gathering around the world."

The reporter glanced behind her before continuing. "We've heard from credible sources that the EMP is only the first strike. More assaults to our country are coming. Some may even hit right here in Los Angeles."

Andy took a step forward, the tan draining from this face.

"W-What Lainey? What sources?" The camera cut away to a man fumbling on a news desk with his hand up to his ear. The elusive Chip. He frowned at what must have been a video feed of the other reporter. "Where are you getting this information?"

The view cut back to Lainey. She pulled an earpiece from her ear like it was a distraction and addressed the camera. "Sources are reporting that the EMP was intended to cause panic and confusion as a cover to buy time. The real attack will be devastating. Everyone needs to listen."

She stepped closer. "Sources report up to twenty-five nuclear bombs are now en route to major cities across the

United States. They could already be here. We don't know when they will detonate or if the government will stop them in time. We—"

The station cut back to the man at the news desk. He plastered on a panicked smile. "We're sorry folks, we're experiencing technical difficulties with Lainey Sinclair's news feed. As soon as we troubleshoot the problem, we will head back out to the Consulate."

He smiled as the station switched camera angles. "Until then, let's go to the lifestyle desk for the recipe of the day."

As Leah stared in shock at the television, the old man pushed out of his chair. He turned the knob and wobbled the rabbit ears and Kramer on *Seinfeld* skittered into view.

"What? No!" Leah stepped forward. "We need to find another news station."

"Your seven minutes are up." The man hobbled back to his worn recliner and flopped into the seat.

"But didn't you hear her? She said more attacks were coming! Nuclear bombs for goodness' sake!"

"I'll believe it when I see it. Now scram."

Leah turned to Andy. He didn't move. She yanked on his arm. "We need to get somewhere safe."

He nodded like his head was floating above his body, disconnected from reality.

Leah stepped toward the old man. "You shouldn't stay here. It's not safe on the top floor with the windows open."

He waved her off. "I'm safe enough."

"You should go to the basement and hide. Take some food and some books. Stay there for a while."

"I'm too old to hide. I'm fine right where I am."

"What if a bomb goes off?"

He rubbed his grimy neck. "If it happens, it happens."

Leah turned to Andy, who still stood there, unable to process what he'd seen and heard. "We need to go."

He nodded again, this time a bit more focused.

Leah spun around, looking at the piles of all the junk. Everything in the place had to be forty years old. Her eyes paused on a key rack above the phone. She turned back to the old man. "Please tell me you have a car."

CHAPTER FIFTEEN

LEAH

Midtown Atlanta

    Saturday, 2:30 p.m.

The garage hid in the back corner of the apartment building, half-basement, half-forgotten concrete hideaway. Tandem parking spaces eked out their existence between support pillars and storage lockers.

Leah held up the old man's keys. When she'd asked if he had a car, he'd waved at the keys like he was pointing down the hall to the bathroom and told her to take them. Leah had stood there, dumbfounded for a minute, until he shouted at her to take the keys and get out. He'd charged ten dollars for seven minutes of television, but then gave them a car?

It made no sense, but neither did his apartment or the fact that he used a battery to watch reruns of a show twenty years off the air. She shook it off. Whatever the reason, she was filled with gratitude. The faded and cracked leather keychain with a Buick logo on top gave her hope. If the car was half as old as the man, they might have a means out of the city.

Leah replayed the reporter's words. A nuclear attack on American soil. Twenty-five bombs. If Atlanta was a target, where would it strike? The Capitol most likely. *Downtown.*

She glanced up at the single window in the garage. It gave a view of the alley and the dumpster outside, but beyond the dented metal container, midtown and downtown cuddled beside each other. If the bomb was as big as the one Andy spoke about, they would be incinerated where they stood or flattened by the collapsing building. They needed to get out of the city.

Leah turned to Andy. He stood by the oversized garage door, staring at the mechanism. He hadn't been in his right mind since watching the TV. She'd dragged him out of that man's apartment and down the stairs to the basement. The whole time, his lips moved with words, but no sound came out.

At some point, he would have to come to grips with reality for his sake. Leah pulled out her phone and checked the battery. Twenty percent. *Not great.* She turned on the flashlight and held it up to inspect the garage.

She found the old man's car in parking space eighteen. An ancient Buick station wagon with wood paneling and more chrome than Leah's bathroom outside the city limits. She stuck the key in the lock and turned. The door barely cleared the nearest pillar.

Brown pleather and the stench of fifty-year-old cigarettes and fast food assaulted her nose. She eased into the driver's seat. A pair of tree air fresheners hung from the rear view and Leah adjusted it for her height.

Here goes nothing.

She stuck the key in the ignition, found the brake pedal, and turned. It cranked and sputtered. *No! Come on.* She pumped the gas like she used to do on her mom's Mercury Sable when she was first learning to drive and tried again.

The engine groaned, teasing her with promise. She waited a minute and tried again. On the fifth turn over the car struggled to life. *Yes!*

Leah leaned forward and rested her head on the enormous steering wheel. They would get out of the city after all. She let the car idle for a few minutes before backing out of the parking space.

As she cranked the wheel harder and harder to the right, she looked around in a panic. What was going on? Her little Chevy back home would be doing wheelies with as much as she'd cranked the wheel. Leah swallowed and tried again, cranking it farther and farther to the right as she managed to turn the car enough to clear the pillar.

She remembered a friend's car years ago when she had just gotten her license. A real beater of a hatchback, it had the same massive wheel and Leah could barely keep it on the road. Her hands had bobbled up and down on the wheel like a little old lady in a cartoon. She looked down at the wheel and it clicked. *No power steering.*

Pressing her hand over her mouth, she thought about the clogged streets and traffic jams all over the city. Would she be able to make it? Could she drive this boat on wheels to Hampton without crashing? Leah cranked the wheel and straightened out. *I don't have a choice. I have to try.*

She put the car in drive and eased up to Andy. As she cranked the window down, Leah stuck her head out. "Figure out how to get the garage door open?"

He still stood in front of the mechanical box bolted to the garage floor. The Buick's headlights broadcast his shadow ten feet tall across the shut metal door. He didn't answer.

"Andy!"

He jumped. "What?"

"The garage door. Can you get it open?"

"Huh? Oh, I don't know." He fished in his pocket and pulled out his crumpled box of cigarettes. He tapped it on his palm. Nothing came out. He peered into the opening.

Leah couldn't take it. Here she was in this death trap on wheels, trying to get them somewhere safe and he was what, taking a smoke break? She shouted. "Andy! We need to get out of here!"

He didn't respond and Leah put the car in park and shoved open the door. The squeak of unused hinges sounded like a scream. She stomped up to the doctor.

"Hey! Wake up!"

He blinked at her. "I'm out of cigarettes."

"You think? You've been smoking like a chimney ever since the blackout. I can't believe they lasted that long."

He brought the pack down and stared at it in his hand. "I need more cigarettes."

"No, you need to get this garage door open so we can get out of here. Bombs, nuclear explosions, death to thousands?" She waved her arms in a circle, imitating a cloud. "Big boom, remember?"

"What's the point? We'll all be incinerated."

"You told me yourself if we get far enough away, we'll survive."

He looked up. "We're in midtown. Any blast will kill us where we stand. We'll be vaporized."

Leah threw up her hands. "Then let's get out of here!"

Andy scratched behind his ear. "You think the old guy smokes? I could go back up, see if he'll sell me some."

Something inside Leah snapped. She couldn't stand there wasting time, trying to convince a doctor of all people to get in the car. Leah wasn't a violent person. She didn't believe in corporal punishment. She volunteered for a local animal rescue. She had never thrown a punch.

But anger and fear coiled low in her belly like a pair of vipers. Andy wasn't going to derail them and she wasn't going to leave him here, standing in a parking garage in midtown, waiting for a bomb to turn him to ash.

Her hand flew out like someone else was in control and her open palm collided with the doctor's cheek. The smack echoed though the garage, louder than the Buick's sputtering engine and the thundering of Leah's heart.

Andy staggered back. "What the hell?"

Leah's hand reddened before her eyes, but she didn't shake it out. The sting gave her clarity. She looked up at Andy. "Focus. We're getting out of here and I need your help to do it."

He held his cheek where she hit him, covering up the fingermarks spreading across his skin. After a moment, he nodded. "What should I do?"

"Get over there and find the garage door handle. I'll see if I can disable the tension rod. You'll need to pull the garage door up."

Andy nodded and walked over to the garage door. He found the handle thanks to the beam of the Buick's headlights. "Ready."

Leah turned back to the gears on the floor. A manual pull-chain with a red handle stuck out from the top and she yanked on it. Something in the gearing shifted. "Try it."

Andy gripped the handle and tugged. The door wobbled and screeched. "It's too heavy."

Leah hurried over to help. Squatting low, she got her hands under the rubber pad on the bottom of the door. They lifted on the count of three. The door shuddered and protested, but together, they forced it open.

Andy staggered back, heaving.

"You lay off the cigarettes and you might be useful after all."

He smiled at the ground, but Leah could tell he was barely hanging on.

She walked over and gave his arm a squeeze. "Just keep it together until we make it to your place, okay? I need you to direct me."

He nodded. "It won't happen again."

Leah held back most of a smirk. "It better not. Because next time, I'll close my fist." She tugged open the driver's door and slid into the seat as Andy hurried around the other side of the car.

He got in the passenger side and groaned. "It smells like something died in here."

"Forty years ago, something probably did." Leah put the Buick in drive and bumped and bounced out of the garage, around the dumpster, and down the alley. The steering wheel felt loose and wobbly in her hands, but she managed to keep from smashing into a wall. "Do you know a back way to your house?"

Andy thought it over. "There's a few. I've gotten creative in rush hour."

"Good, because with all the cars stalled on the major roads, we'll need a miracle."

He pointed at the nearest cross-street. "Turn left and then take the second right. We'll run parallel to the highway as best we can."

Leah nodded and followed his directions, white-knuckling every turn. The car shuddered as she spun the oversized wheel. She glanced at Andy with a grimace. "I'll get the hang of it eventually."

He held up his hands. "I drive a Fiat. It's the size of

the backseat and turns on a dime. I wouldn't have been able to back this thing up."

"It wasn't easy." Leah lapsed into silence as she concentrated on driving.

With every mile, her confidence behind the wheel grew, but their progression slowed. Andy pointed out where to turn and gave her alternatives when the road ahead became too congested to make it. They crawled out of midtown at a snail's pace.

Leah drove over a curb to avoid a solid wall of stalled cars. A woman stood inside the doorway of the closest building, staring with an open mouth. It wasn't the first time. So far, they hadn't run into any serious trouble. A couple of kids followed them for a while, racing and shouting down the street until Leah lost them, but that was all.

If someone with bad intentions heard the car, she didn't know if they would be so lucky. Thankfully, the farther they drove, the nicer the neighborhood became. In the last mile, they traded commercial buildings and strip malls for brick colonials and grass front yards.

Andy pointed at another street and scooted forward as they turned the corner. It was the entrance to a newer subdivision, filled with craftsman-styled houses bunched together like sardines in a tin. He bent to peer out the windshield. "See the yellow house on the left, four down?"

Leah nodded.

"Turn in there."

"That's your place?"

He nodded.

Leah took stock of all the houses. Neat and tidy with little flower beds around the mailboxes and newer cars in the driveways. All new construction, not more than five years old. She crossed her fingers as she asked a question. "Do any of these houses have basements?"

Andy's face fell. "No. They're all on slabs."

Leah nodded and pulled into Andy's driveway. They would need to find somewhere else to hide.

As she put the car in park, the front door to the house flew open. A redhead in athletic wear rushed from the house. She stopped in the driveway as soon as she spotted Andy.

Even inside the car, Leah could hear the woman's tone as she pointed and shouted.

"Who is that?"

Andy winced. "My wife."

CHAPTER SIXTEEN

GRANT

Rural South Carolina
    Saturday, 1:00 p.m.

Grant tapped the gas gauge for the tenth time. The needle hovered on the E for empty. Cursing himself, he wiped his mouth with the back of his hand before looking around. He was in the middle of nowhere.

No houses. No little towns. No gas stations.

When he ran out of map, Grant thought he could manage by street signs and follow the state roads through South Carolina and into Georgia. It wasn't that easy. The signs claimed this was a state road, but it wasn't getting him anywhere fast.

For all he knew, a town could be just over the next rise or forty miles to his west or east. He stared out at the wire fencing separating the scrabble on the side of the road from the pasture beyond. Someone owned these fields, but who?

Farms had gas for their tractors and other equipment. If he could only see a house. Grant leaned forward, squinting into the distance when the car sputtered. *Oh, no. Not yet.* He pumped the gas pedal.

The car coughed and the engine died. Grant coasted over to the weeds and put the Cutlass in park. He rested his head on the cracked steering wheel.

I'm never going to make it home in time. He pulled out his phone. *No service.* He stared at the picture of his wife he used as a background and almost lost it. Tears pricked his eyes and he snuffed back a storm of snot. *Please get out of the city. Please make it somewhere safe.*

If the bombs went off before he could find her, it might take weeks to track her down. Months, even. Grant didn't know much about nuclear bombs apart from what he remembered reading about in high school history class. Vague terms like fallout and radiation clung to him, but the details were too sketchy to recall.

He sat back and sucked in a breath before wiping at his face. Giving up now wasn't an option. If he couldn't drive to Atlanta, he would walk. Walking was only a setback, not a death sentence. He would find his wife.

Grant moved to shove his phone back in his pocket, but stopped. He pulled open the services section and moved to cellular. The phone searched for service, but it came up empty. He scrolled to Wi-Fi. He knew the odds were a million to one, maybe worse, but as the little wheel turned looking for signal... He prayed.

A single Wi-Fi network appeared. *Dueling Banjos.* Signal strength, one bar. He tried to connect. It prompted him for a password. Grant looked up. Somewhere near him, someone had power.

He clambered out of the car and held the phone up to the sky. Still one bar. He walked ten paces and waited; the signal didn't improve. Pulling the phone down, Grant spun in a circle. Trees and pasture all around. He would need to hunt.

Grant set the phone on the roof and tugged open the back door of the Cutlass. After rooting around in his suitcase, he pulled out a drawstring bag he used for carrying his gym gear when he traveled.

He dumped out the sweatbands and little bottles of shampoo and filled it with the two bottles of Gatorade he had left and the three Power Bars. They would get him through today, even if he spent the majority of it hiking through the fields of South Carolina.

Grant grabbed the shotgun and took a deep breath. Then he took his phone, swiped it open again, and went on the hunt.

Sticking to the road, he hiked north the way he came, stopping every hundred yards to check the reception. When the network disappeared, he turned around and backtracked.

He passed the Cutlass and kept on going over a hill and down the other side. The network disappeared again about three hundred yards south of the Cutlass. Grant cursed and ran a hand through his hair.

If the signal wasn't coming from somewhere on the

road, he'd have to traipse through the fields. It meant trespassing and poor visibility and the risk of walking into something he couldn't walk out of.

Some people chose to live in the middle of the country because they didn't like interlopers. If he ran into one of them, he might never make it home. Grant checked the shotgun he'd lifted from the kid in the gas station.

Four shells, pump action. A solid defensive weapon with good stopping power. But four shells wouldn't go far. He hiked back to the Cutlass and stood beside the front fender.

Leah needed him. He stared at the field in front of him and shrugged out of his jacket. He laid it across the wire and used it as a shield to climb over without snagging his skin. A cut from a jagged barbed-wire spike could bring anything from staph to tetanus. He couldn't risk it.

After easing through, Grant slipped his jacket back on, slung the bag over his shoulder, and set off. He rested the shotgun on the hollow between his shoulder and clavicle, securing it with his arm as he held the phone out in front of him.

The pasture lands were two or three years fallow, with occasional shafts of renegade wheat dried and decaying amongst the weeds. He walked due west, following the afternoon sun. The land rose ahead of him, cresting in a ridge line with oak trees and shade.

In the summer months, cows would congregate beneath the branches for shade, but on this cold January day, no animals roamed about. Grant reached the top of the rise and stood beneath the largest tree.

The wind chilled his hands and he took a moment to warm them. Ahead, fields stretched out in a patchwork sea. It was the epitome of rural America. Farmlands and tranquility and not a high-rise or traffic jam in sight.

Grant thought about his job back home and his frenetic day-to-day living. He married Leah five years before, but only now were they seriously discussing kids. It had seemed impossible before. First she needed to finish nursing school and he needed a stable job. Then it was overtime and unpredictable shifts and travel two out of every six weeks. They couldn't even manage a dog. And now what? Now that the threat of an attack loomed in Grant's mind, he wished he'd made different choices.

He grew up in a little farm town with a handful of kids his age and a single elementary school for the entire county. Now he lived among millions of people and sat in traffic and flipped radio stations and never sat still.

His days were filled with computer software and technology conferences and flights halfway across the country. If he'd stayed in his hometown, he'd never have met his wife. But now they were about to be torn apart.

A pain lodged in his chest and Grant turned back to his phone and waited as the Wi-Fi networks populated. Dueling Banjos appeared with two bars.

Grant jerked his head up looked around. He was headed in the right direction.

He navigated down the hill and through another

fence line and section of forest. The signal remained steady.

Half an hour of plodding through mud and dirt and fallen leaves, he emerged at yet another fence line and a dirt road. Grant clambered through the fence and stopped in the middle of the track. The signal had to be close. He squinted into the distance. Something shimmered in the descending sunlight.

Loping ahead, Grant stopped at a narrow, paved road. *This must be it.* To his left, the road stretched back up over the hill where he'd come from. To his right, it dipped down into another valley. Something stood beside the road at the edge of his vision.

Grant hustled to it, squinting until it came clear. A mailbox.

He almost whooped for joy and took off running. It was a rural box, made of dull metal and shaped to slough off snow. Grant stopped beside it. A gravel road connected to the pavement just past the mailbox.

The signal strength on his phone jumped to full strength at three. He held a hand up to shield his view from the dipping sun. A gate stood twenty feet down, shutting off access to the gravel. A sign reading *No Trespassing* was lashed to the wooden cross-bar.

Grant stared at it. He needed to trespass. It was the only way to find help. But he didn't want to be shot at, either. He set down his bag and thought it over. Only one idea came to him.

He slipped off his jacket and sweatshirt and long-sleeved T-shirt before tugging his white undershirt over his head. He tied the stinky thing to the end of the shotgun and redressed before grabbing his bag.

With the shotgun held high and the white shirt waving like a flag in the wind, Grant approached the gate.

CHAPTER SEVENTEEN

GRANT

Rural South Carolina
   Saturday, 3:00 p.m.

After easing under the wood crossbeams, Grant made his way down the well-maintained gravel road. As the road bent to the right, a blue South Carolina flag came into view. It waved atop a flagpole in front of what could only be described as a rustic mansion.

With full scribe log walls, solar panels covering the entire roof, and what looked to be a massive well beside it, the home had it all. As Grant stood and stared, a terrific barking sounded from around the back of the house.

A ball of fur and speed raced around the far side of the building and Grant backed up a step. A huge German shepherd closed the distance between Grant and the house, barking with every leap.

Grant loved dogs. He'd lost his golden retriever a year before and hadn't had the heart to replace her. A friendly lap dog until the end, Sage spent her last night snuggled up against Grant's leg on the couch.

The dog running at him wasn't friendly. If it got close enough to Grant's lap, it would take a bite out of it, not sleep against it. Grant didn't know what to do. Running would be worse; he'd become prey. He wouldn't shoot it.

All he could do was stand there and hope it didn't maul him. Grant braced himself for the attack when a whistle cut the dog's bark in two. The dog collapsed in a crouch fifteen feet away. It focused on Grant, waiting.

The front door of the house opened and a man stepped out, wearing jeans and a plaid shirt made for tough winter labor. He eased off the porch and approached Grant, shotgun of his own in his hands.

He stopped beside the dog. "Can't you read?"

Grant waved the white shirt.

"Unless you want a window in your middle, I would put that weapon on the ground."

Grant set the shotgun down and stood, hands up in surrender. "I need help."

"Obviously." The man's beard twitched. "Only an idiot would traipse onto my land with a shotgun and expect to stay alive."

The dog growled and Grant nodded. "You're right and I apologize. But I'm lost and I ran out of gas out on Route 81."

From the distance, Grant couldn't gauge the stranger's age, but it couldn't have been much older than

Grant. His arms bulged with hard work's reward and he squinted as he spoke. "Don't see how that's my problem."

"No, it's not." Grant swallowed. "But I'm hoping to buy some gas and directions. I can pay."

"Money's no good here."

"I can work."

The man glanced down at the dog and said something Grant couldn't hear. The dog advanced.

"I don't want any trouble!"

"Layla will decide that. Put the bag on the ground, too."

Grant did as instructed. The dog trotted up, nose working overtime. She sniffed his track pants and sneakers before turning to his bag and finally the shotgun. She trotted back to the man and resumed her place by his side.

"Did I pass?"

The man's lips thinned. "Yes. Where are you headed?"

"Atlanta. My wife is there. I need to find her."

He stared at Grant for a long time, but at last he conceded. "Fine. I've got some cement mix around back. You move it to the barn and I'll give you enough gas to get home."

"And directions?"

"You do a decent enough job and we'll talk."

"Thank you." Grant nodded and stepped forward, but the man held up a hand.

"Don't do anything stupid. I don't want to clean up the mess when I shoot you."

Grant swallowed and glanced at the sun. Time was precious, but at least now he had a chance.

The man turned around with the dog at his side and headed back toward the house. He stopped at the porch. "You coming or what?"

Grant bent to pick up his shotgun.

"Leave it."

He complied and hurried to catch up. Following the man around the side of the house, they entered the working portion of the farm complete with three outbuildings, a mass of farm equipment, and a brand-new Ford F-150 that probably would never run again.

The man lowered the tailgate to the truck. There had to be twenty bags of cement mix inside, each one weighing fifty pounds.

Grant swallowed down a groan. "Where do you want them?"

"In the far barn along the east wall. You'll see the place."

Grant shrugged out of his jacket and set to work, picking up the first dust-covered bag and hoisting it up to his shoulder. He ran-walked the hundred yards to the far barn and eased inside.

A space sat cleared and ready along the wall between hay bales and a locking metal cabinet. Grant dropped the first bag and hustled back to the truck. The man didn't say a word. He stood beside the truck with a clear view of Grant the entire way, shotgun resting on his forearm. The dog stayed by his side.

Thirty minutes later, Grant dumped the last bag

inside the barn and almost collapsed from exhaustion. Sweat ran down his face and dribbled off his nose and he leaned against a support beam to catch his breath.

"You all right?"

Grant nodded. "Tired and thirsty, that's all."

"Hungry, too?"

"Sure am."

The man jerked his head toward the house. "You can come in and shower off if you like. I can grab you something to eat." He stuck out his hand. "Logan Sullivan."

Grant pushed off the post and gave Logan's hand a shake. "Grant Walton. Thank you for your kindness."

"Don't see how asking you to move a thousand pounds of cement mix is kind, but whatever tickles your fancy." He pointed toward the house. "Shower's down the main hall. Second door on the left."

Grant blinked. "Aren't you coming?"

"After I clean up out here."

Grant nodded and hurried to the house, taking the back stairs two at a time. He pushed the back door open and stepped inside. The place was even bigger on the inside with soaring ceilings and a kitchen that took up the entire back wall. Grant slipped off his dirty shoes and crossed a living room big enough for ten people before finding the bathroom.

After a quick shower, he toweled off, dragged his sweaty clothes back on with a grimace and headed to the kitchen.

Logan stood at the counter putting the top on a

sandwich piled with meat and cheese and lettuce. He glanced up as Grant came in. "Sandwich?"

Grant checked his watch. He needed to go, but his stomach practically leapt out of his throat. He'd be no good to Leah if he passed out. "That would be great, thanks."

Logan offered a seat at the kitchen table and Grant wolfed the sandwich and a bag of chips down before guzzling a glass of water.

"Thank you again." He leaned back in the chair. "You've got an impressive setup here. Is it all off the grid?"

"One hundred percent. I've been self-sufficient for three years now."

Grant swallowed. "Have you heard what's happened?"

"The EMP?" Logan nodded. "High-altitude ballistic missile launched off the East Coast. Probably from a cargo ship."

Grant sat up with a start. "Are you getting the news? TV channels?"

"Nope. Got that all from the ham."

Grant raised an eyebrow. "Your pigs are reporters?"

Logan chuckled and pushed off the counter. "No. The ham radio. Come on, I'll show you, then we can fill up your car."

Grant followed Logan to an office tucked in the corner of the house. A bank of radio equipment sat between two windows looking out on the front of the property. "Even with an EMP, radios still work. Ham radio culture has dwindled over the last forty years, but there's still a good number of truckers who use it."

"And you can communicate with them?"

Logan nodded. "With a big enough antenna and the right atmospheric conditions, I can reach California."

Grant's mouth fell open. "What have you heard?"

"The whole East Coast is dark. Cars are stalled out all over the roads. The cities are in chaos, but without transportation, there's not a lot people can do."

Grant ran a hand down his face. "Have you heard about any more threats?"

"The bombs?"

"Nuclear bombs. Twenty-five of them targeting the largest cities."

Logan nodded again. "That's what I've heard. But no one knows if it's true."

"Are you going to do anything? Take any precautions?"

"The way I figure it, I've done all that already. I'm here, a hundred miles from any target, with enough food and water to keep me going. What else do I need?"

"Are you all alone?"

Logan smiled. "That's where my hospitality ends." He walked to the door. "Let's see to that gas."

Grant respected the hell out of a man who took care of himself and whatever family he was protecting. A pang of jealousy hit him low, but he shoved it down and followed Logan to a tank filled with gasoline.

Logan pulled a red portable gas can from the closest barn and filled it up. He handed it over to Grant. "You'll want to follow Route 81 south. It'll seem like you aren't going anywhere, but eventually, you'll hit Highway 72. Turn west and you'll cross the water into Georgia. There's a town not too far across the border."

"Thank you."

"You're welcome."

Grant wanted to say more, but the pull of his wife kept his mouth shut. He turned to hurry back to his car when the dog from his arrival appeared. She scampered up and licked the back of his hand.

Logan chuckled. "Guess she really does like you."

Grant smiled and hurried off, stopping only to grab his jacket, bag, and shotgun. He loped down the gravel drive, careful not to slosh the gas inside the tank. It took him over half an hour to retrace his steps back to the Cutlass. He filled the tank, put the empty can in the trunk, and fell into the driver's seat.

He pumped the gas pedal and touched the starter wires together. The car protested. He fought back the urge to break something and tried again. The Cutlass started on the third attempt.

Grant exhaled and put the car in drive. *Hang on, Leah. I'm coming.*

CHAPTER EIGHTEEN

LEAH

Buckhead Atlanta
  Saturday, 4:00 p.m.

Marley Phillips hadn't stopped screaming since they pulled into the driveway five minutes before.

"You think it's safe to get out yet?"

Andy shook his head. "Not until she stops gesticulating. If she's still got the energy to point, she's dangerous."

Leah laughed despite the scene. "You do love each other, right?"

"Madly. Can't you tell?"

Andy's wife paused on the lawn, her chest heaving and cheeks flaming to match her hair. When she started in again, she kept her hands on her hips. Andy clapped and reached for the door handle. "There we go. She's tired herself out."

Leah stopped him. "What's she like to be called?"

"What?"

"Your wife. You said don't call her Marley. So what should I call her?"

Andy grinned. "I'll let her tell you." He stepped out of the car, a huge smile on his face. "Babe, it's okay." He threw his arms wide and his wife stared at him like he'd offered her a gastric bypass.

She nodded at Leah still sitting in the car.

Andy motioned for her to come out and Leah obliged, sliding out of the driver's seat on shaky legs. The stress of driving the ancient Buick through miles of abandoned vehicles and prying eyes tapped her strength. She wobbled over to Andy and his wife.

"This is Leah Walton. She's a nurse at Georgia Memorial. If it weren't for her, I wouldn't be here."

Andy's wife stared at Leah, scrutinizing her from head to toe. At last, she stuck out her hand. "Mimi Phillips."

Leah shook her hand. "Hi."

"I suppose he wants me to thank you."

Leah tucked a loose strand of hair behind her ear. "I was headed this way anyway."

Mimi tilted her head. "You live around here?"

"No." Leah chewed on her lip. "My sister lives in Hampton. My husband is meeting me there."

At the mention of her husband, Mimi's gaze landed on Leah's wedding band. She softened. "Have you talked to him?"

"No. Grant left me a ton of messages, but with the phones down, I can't return the call."

Mimi nodded and turned to her husband. "That's how I felt these past two days. Not able to reach you, no calls, no texts. I've been going out of my mind."

The two fluffy white dogs at Andy's feet barked in agreement.

"So have Tinker and Bell."

Leah glanced down at the little dogs before looking back up. She mouthed their names to Andy.

He shrugged and turned to his wife. "You know I tried to call, but with everything down, it was impossible. We even talked to a guy from the phone company."

"You did? For me?"

Leah didn't bother to correct Mimi's assumption. She bent down to pet the dogs instead.

Andy broke the silence. "Hon, I think we need to go inside. There's some things we need to talk about."

"Like why our car won't work or the lights aren't on? Or how you ate the last of the granola bars and left the empty box in the pantry?"

Andy leaned in to give his wife a kiss. She pushed him away. "You stink like an ashtray! Have you been smoking?" Mimi turned to Leah. "Has he been smoking?"

Leah swallowed. "The last day's been really stressful."

Mimi threw up her hands and stalked into the house, shouting obscenities to no one in particular.

Andy stuck his nose in his shirt and inhaled. "Do I really smell that bad?"

"Depends on how much you like smoke, I guess."

He motioned toward the house. "Come on in and rest for a while. Get something to eat. It's going to be dark soon. You'll need your wits about you."

Leah looked back at the Buick. "I have a long way to go."

Andy reached for her. "I need your help telling Mimi the rest. She's not going to take the news well."

"The bomb threat?"

Andy nodded. "Please, Leah. You'll help keep her calm."

Leah stood on the edge of the driveway, staring up at Andy's house. She needed to leave. Thoughts of her husband and her sister and the worry that must be consuming them dominated her thoughts. But Andy needed help, too.

If his wife didn't come to terms with what might be coming, they wouldn't be ready. The threat of a nuclear attack could be hanging over their heads for days, weeks, even. Or it could happen in an instant. The sooner Mimi prepared, the better.

"Okay. But I'm leaving within the hour, so talk fast."

Andy agreed and ushered her into the house. Tinker and Bell scurried in with them, yipping at Leah's heels.

They found Mimi in the kitchen, practically gulping a glass of wine. Andy didn't hold back. "The blackout wasn't caused by a freak storm or a malfunction at the power plant."

Mimi set her glass down. "Seeing as the cars are all

stalled, except for the one you magically showed up in, I figured as much."

"It was a nuclear bomb."

Mimi paled. "What? Where?"

"Detonated high in the atmosphere. It caused an EMP."

Andy let Leah explain what she knew thanks to the crazy patient in the ER. When she finished, he waved at her to keep talking. Leah tucked her hair behind her ear even though none was out of place. "The same patient claimed it was only the first strike. That more bombs would follow."

"More high-altitude ones?"

"No. This time on the ground."

Andy's wife shook her head. "I don't follow. Are you telling me we're at risk for nuclear war?"

"Basically, yes." Andy stepped forward. "We found the car thanks to a man who rigged up a boat battery to his TV. He let us watch a few minutes of a news broadcast out of Los Angeles."

Andy faltered and Leah stepped in, finishing the story. "The reporter corroborated what my patient said and what I could parse out from my husband's messages. There are twenty-five nuclear bombs in play targeting the top cities in the United States."

"Including here?"

Leah nodded. "Atlanta is one of the targets, yes."

Mimi eased down to a kitchen stool. "So that's it? We get hit with an EMP and the government can't protect us? What about the military or the police? Where are they? Why aren't they evacuating?"

Andy reached for his wife's hand. "I'm not sure local police departments know. We ran into a pair of city cops and they didn't believe us."

Leah shook her head in dismay, remembering the dead man and the cop's dismissal. "Not one bit."

"But the federal government... The FBI... CIA... someone has to know."

"Doesn't mean they can stop it." Leah plucked at her sleeve. "I'm sure they've at least heard the rumors. They probably knew about it days ago. But what if they can't find the source? What if they don't know where the bombs are or who's setting them off?"

Mimi ran a hand over her hair. "How big a bomb are we talking about? Can it fit in a suitcase or does it have to be carted in on a tractor-trailer?"

Andy glanced up at the ceiling, trying to remember. "I think I've got it in a book in the office. Hold on." He scrambled out of the room, reappearing a second later. He flipped the pages on a large paperback until he found the right section.

"This says the bomb dropped on Hiroshima would fit in the back of a small delivery truck or maybe even a van."

Leah swallowed. "You mean one of those white delivery vans we see on every street downtown?"

Andy closed the book and nodded.

"Trying to track down twenty-five vans in cities

teeming with millions of people would be impossible." Leah ran a hand over her forehead. "We don't know how long this has been planned or who's responsible. For all we know, the bombs could have been here for years, waiting."

Andy opened the book again and rifled through the pages. "This says that decommissioned nuclear weapons are held in various levels of security. The US keeps the best track, but Russia is the worst."

He looked up with wide eyes. "There are some facilities in northern Russia that don't have security at all."

"What? Give me that." Andy's wife snatched the book and read the two open pages. When she looked up, her face confirmed Andy's words. "It's hopeless. We're all going to die."

"No, that's not true." Leah leaned across the counter. "Even if a bomb goes off, we can survive."

Andy agreed. "We're far enough out of the blast radius here that the initial impact won't kill us."

"But what about radiation?"

"We'll need to find shelter. Preferably somewhere with a basement."

Mimi took another gulp of wine. "For how long?"

Andy glanced at Leah. "Up to two weeks."

His wife snorted out a laugh. "Yeah, right. Where are we going to find a basement we can crash in for two weeks?"

Leah spoke up. "Isn't there anywhere in the neighborhood?"

Andy scratched his head. "Doesn't the community building have something?"

Mimi's brows knitted. "I think you're right. When we first moved in, they planned to make it two stories with an exit from the bottom to the pool."

Andy brightened. "You're right. When the plans were redrawn, the developer filled that area in to make a playground." He spun to Leah with hope on his face for the first time in hours. "The basement's got to be there. We just need to find a way in."

Mimi stood up. "I'll go find Becky. She's on the homeowners' association. She'll know."

Leah turned to Andy. "While she's figuring it out, you need to pack."

"What for?"

"Your impromptu trip to basement paradise. All of you need to find that basement and get in it. Those bombs could go off any minute."

"What about you?"

"I need to find my sister."

Andy reached out and rested his hand on Leah's shoulder. "Thank you for bringing me home."

She smiled. "You're welcome."

As Leah turned to leave, shouts erupted outside. She glanced at Andy. "Now what?"

CHAPTER NINETEEN

LEAH

Buckhead Atlanta
Saturday, 4:30 p.m.

Andy rushed outside and Leah followed.

A man stood on Andy's driveway, gesticulating at the car. "I don't know, Mimi, you tell me. How the hell did you get a working car?"

"It's not my car!" Mimi shouted back as Andy rushed to stand between them.

He held up his hands. "Hi, Tom. What's the trouble?"

The larger man hoisted up his belt and pointed again. "Your wife comes over babbling about how we're all about to be nuked to smithereens, I come out here, and you've got a car in your driveway. How'd you get it to work?"

Andy shook his head. "The car doesn't matter. What

matters is the threat. Mimi's right. There could be another attack anytime."

Tom screwed up his face like he just chomped on a rotten pickle. "Another attack? Where did you hear that? A little voice in your head?"

Andy's shoulders bunched. "No. The television."

Tom took a step forward. "You've got a working TV? How?"

Leah eased into the conversation. She couldn't stand there while this neighbor all but accosted Andy. "We ran into a man who used some ingenuity and a battery." She folded her arms across her chest. "What Andy says is true. There are reports out of Los Angeles that a nuclear attack is coming. You need to take shelter."

A woman hurried out from a house across the street, blonde hair up in a messy bun. She stopped beside Tom. "Honey, stop badgering Andy. Mimi's just taking precautions."

Tom didn't even look at his wife. "She's stirring up panic, is what she's doing."

The woman gave a placating smile in Andy's direction. "What if she's right? I mean this blackout is strange."

"It's got to have an explanation. There's no way we're under attack. This is the United States for God's sake."

"Doesn't mean it can't happen. We've been bombed before."

"Yeah, by a guy with a homemade bomb in the back of his truck or in a backpack. Not a nuclear bomb. That's war."

Leah didn't say anything. She thought about what the reporter said on TV and how the network cut her feed in the middle of her warning. Did the government know who was responsible? Were they covering it up?

The West Coast must be in the grips of a widespread panic. If the news of the potential bombs was hitting television networks and internet media, then every city from Los Angeles and San Francisco to Seattle and Portland would be knee-deep in chaos. Traffic jams. Looting. Mass riots and violence.

She narrowed her eyes as Tom snorted in Andy's direction. Neighbors turning on neighbors.

"Where are they launching from? North Korea?"

Andy answered with reluctance. "We don't know."

Tom shook his head. "Leave it to an emergency-room doctor to spread lies and panic."

"What's that supposed to mean?"

"You heard me." Tom puffed out his chest. "You're always going on about some risk or another. Last week it was the flu, this week it's nuclear attack. You sound like a broken record."

"Honey, please." The woman tugged on her husband's arm, but he shoved her off.

Leah tried to keep the rising anger out of her voice. "This isn't made up. I watched the same news report. I talked to a patient in the ER who confirmed it. The blackout wasn't from an accident or a storm. It was an EMP from a nuclear missile detonated up in the atmosphere."

"What? Are you saying this wasn't an accident?" A

woman Leah hadn't noticed rushed up from across the street and a handful of other neighbors followed. It was turning into a crowd.

She nodded. "I think so, yes."

Murmurs rushed through the adults. A child tugged on a woman's shirt. "Mommy, I'm scared."

The woman hoisted the little girl of three or four up into her arms. "It's okay, Anna."

"If only that were true." Leah had to convince these people to take precautions.

Tom snorted. "You're inciting a panic and we don't even know who you are."

Andy held out his hand. "Her name is Leah Walton. She's an emergency-room nurse with me at Georgia Memorial."

Leah glanced down at her scrubs. At least she could corroborate that. "I know it's a shock, but please. Everyone needs to listen."

"Does anyone know if we can access the basement of the community center?" Andy addressed Tom's wife. "Becky, you're on the HOA, do you know?"

She nodded. "I'm pretty sure we can through the main floor. But I don't think it's finished. The plans were changed before the building was built out. It might just be concrete."

Andy nodded. "Concrete is good. The more between us and the atmosphere, the better."

A person in the gathering crowd called out. "For what?"

"Fallout. We don't want to be outside when the bomb

goes off. We're close enough to be inside the radiation plume."

More murmurs, more heads shaking in disbelief.

"This isn't the Cold War! We're safe. No one can attack us here."

Leah understood the reluctance to accept the horror of the situation, but she'd heard it enough to believe it. First the texts and messages from her husband, then the man in the ER and the burn victim on the street. The reporter confirmed it before her feed was cut.

She frowned. Some of the people shouting and talking and clutching their children had a point. Why weren't there emergency alerts? She pulled out her phone. No service. Maybe they couldn't get through.

Leah counted the hours. Almost seventeen since the man from the phone company told her about the cell towers. She had no reason to doubt his veracity. If the generators powering the working cell towers up and down the East Coast only had enough fuel for eight hours, then they ran out a long time ago.

For all they knew, alerts were going out all over the West Coast and people were hunkering down and preparing for the worst. They just couldn't receive them in Atlanta.

She exhaled through her mouth. The longer they stayed outside, the more at risk they became. "All right!" Leah put on her nurse voice and cupped her hands around her mouth to project across the street. "All those interested, pack food, clothes, things to do. Anything you would want with you for a week underground."

Andy's neighbors fell silent and he filled the void. "Head to the community center. It will be the safest place to wait out the attack."

"What if we can't get in?"

"What if the bombs hit?"

"What about my parents across town?"

"My daughter's at a friend's house!"

Leah held up her hands against the rising panic. "Andy will figure out a way into the basement at the community center. I can't help with the rest."

Tom's voice boomed out. "What if we don't want to listen to a couple of crazy people?"

Andy shook his head. "You can come or not. No one is going to force you."

Tom turned to his wife. "Come on, Becky. I'm tired of listening to these nuts."

Becky hesitated. "What about the boys, Tom?"

He fixed her with a stare. "We aren't going."

She nodded. "All right."

Watching the exchange between Tom and his wife spiked Leah's blood pressure. If she wanted to come, that was her choice. Her husband could stay outside and absorb enough radiation for both of them.

As Becky turned to go, she glanced up at Leah.

"Come." Leah mouthed the word, but Becky got it. She nodded before hurrying away.

Leah leaned closer to Andy. "I don't like that guy."

"Join the club."

Mimi ran up to them, out of breath and panting. "I've told everyone I can down the street. Mary promised to tell everyone on the next street over. Brian's hitting the rest of the neighborhood."

"Do you think people will come?"

Mimi wiped the sheen of sweat off her brow. "Honestly? I don't know. Half of them looked at me like I'd done too many drugs this morning."

"The other half?"

"Probably losing it in their kitchens right now."

Panic was better than apathy or denial. Leah motioned toward the house. "You need to get your things and get down there."

Andy paused. "You should come with us."

"I can't. I have to get to my sister's place."

"Are you sure?" Mimi palmed her hips as she struggled to regain her breath. "We could use a level head like yours around here."

"I know." Leah turned back around and surveyed the street. Five houses down a couple ushered two small children out the front door with bags on their backs and a rolling wagon filled with food. At least they were being cautious.

The helper in her wanted to stay and get as many people to safety as possible. Leah grimaced with the weight of her decision. "I can't. My sister needs me and my husband's probably frantic with worry."

Andy reached out and wrapped Leah up in a surprise hug. She inhaled against his shirt and launched into a coughing fit.

"You should probably change before you go. Mimi's right, you do smell like an ashtray."

Andy chuckled and pulled back. "Take care of yourself, Nurse Walton."

"You, too, Doctor Phillips." Leah smiled at both Andy and his wife before hurrying to the car.

She slid into the driver's seat and slammed the door. There was no time to waste.

After starting the engine, Leah put the car in reverse and gripped the back of the seat. Tom stood across the street in his yard, arms folded and staring. She backed out and bumped over the sidewalk in front of his house.

As she put the car in drive, Leah faced forward. Tom and his doubt hovered in the rearview until she turned the corner and left Andy's subdivision behind.

CHAPTER TWENTY

LEAH

North Atlanta

Saturday, 5:25 p.m.

The thousandth stalled car blocked Leah's route and she eased over the sidewalk and around it. With one eye on the clock and the other on the setting sun, she kept the car pointing northwest as best as possible. The sun slipped below the horizon and Leah frowned. In twenty minutes or so, she would be forced to use the headlights.

Obstacles would be harder to avoid and without a map, getting lost would be easy. The fifty-year-old car didn't come with a compass. Finding her way to Hampton would be difficult.

I could stop for the night. Leah slowed and took stock of the area. Houses set back from the road, the occasional family out in the front yard playing tag or riding scooters in their driveways. A typical day.

She wanted to shout at them, force them all inside and somewhere safe. But she wasn't safe. She was out on the road trying to outrun impending disaster. Leah glanced at a street sign as she crossed an intersection. How far from downtown had she traveled?

Eight miles? Ten? She didn't know. Was she even out of the range of the blast?

Stopping for the night crossed her mind, but she pushed it away. She couldn't take the time. Her sister Dawn needed her. Grant needed her. She would drive all night to Hampton if that's what it took.

As she turned onto a larger road with four lanes and a median in the middle, she exhaled. It was a straight shot north and relatively free of cars. Small favors. As Leah accelerated, she traded rows of houses for entrances to subdivisions and stand-alone restaurants and coffee shops on corners.

She crested the top of a hill and everything changed.

The back window of the Buick exploded in light. Brilliant, white hot, and searing, it engulfed the car, spreading out in all directions.

Leah slammed on the brakes and squeezed her eyes shut. What the...? She put the car in park and scrambled down beneath the seat as reality flooded her brain.

Oh God. No. Please, no.

Her eyelids glowed red, light overwhelming everything. *This is it. It's happening.* With her arms over her head, she curled up into a ball. *Please stop. Please stop.*

She sobbed and begged for relief. *Don't let me*

incinerate. Please. I need to live. I need to be there for Grant and Dawn. I need to help people survive.

As she rocked back and forth on the seat, a rolling boom, larger than any rumble of thunder, shook the car and rattled Leah's bones. It was all true. The threat. The attack. The bombs going off.

Her eyes still burned with light, but it faded in intensity. She risked blinking. Spots swam in her vision, but the blinding light was gone. She sat up. *I'm not dead. I'm still alive.*

She patted herself all over. What did Andy say? Radiation took twenty minutes to fall? Was that it?

Leah couldn't remember. Panic swelled up in her belly, roiling her empty stomach and shooting shivers down her limbs. She had to find cover. Somewhere with a basement or thick walls of concrete. What had he said? The more concrete, the better. She glanced at her watch: 5:35.

She gripped the steering wheel with trembling hands, put the car in drive, and punched the gas. Subdivisions sped by. Little coffee shops made of wood frame and drywall. Nothing substantial. Nothing thick enough to save her.

There had to be something, somewhere.

A man stood on the grass of his corner lot and Leah slowed. He thrust his hands in front of him and waved them about like Frankenstein's monster in an old horror movie. As he stumbled, she hit the gas.

He was blind.

Oh my God. If I hadn't ducked... If I had stared at the

light, I wouldn't be able to see. She pushed the accelerator to the floor, scraping the bottom of the car across the sidewalk as she bounced over it to avoid abandoned cars, sideswiping bushes and mailboxes.

Where can I go? Where will be safe? She gunned it through another intersection. Side streets gave way to small strip malls. Maybe one of them would have a basement? But would it be enough? Would she be able to get in?

She turned into the first parking lot, front fender screeching as it caught on the sidewalk. It didn't matter. If she didn't get to shelter, the car would be a worthless accessory. A massive two-story Barnes & Noble with oversized wood and glass doors sat back off the street. The walls were made of concrete.

It would have to do.

Leah slammed the car in park, taking up half the parking spaces in the row.

She checked the time: 5:40. *I have to hurry.*

Scrambling into the back seat, Leah grabbed her bag. She threw the driver's door open and almost fell out of the car. Leah ran to the store, tripping over the curb and almost sprawling out on her face. As she stumbled upright, she grabbed the door handle. It didn't budge.

"No! Let me in!" She slammed her fists on the glass, pounding for someone to hear her. "I need help!" Her shouts turned to sobs. "I can't die out here. I can't."

She heaved and leaned against the door, exhausted already. There had to be another way inside. Pushing off the locked front door, Leah ran around to the back. A metal service door sat up three steps. She rushed to it and tried the handle. *Locked.*

She banged on it with her foot, kicking as hard as possible. *No response.*

Tears streamed down her face and clouded her vision. Snot in her throat made it hard to breathe. *This can't be the end.* She checked the time: 5:44.

Ten minutes since the blast. *I'm running out of time.*

She ran back to the Buick. Driving somewhere else wasn't an option. The bookstore had concrete walls and two stories' worth of material to absorb the radiation. It was her best option. She had to get inside. Leah popped the trunk and yanked out the tire iron.

I can do this.

Rushing back to the front of the store, she picked the window farthest from the doors and closest to the bookshelves. She summoned all her strength, gripped the tire iron in her fist, and swung.

The glass cracked, splinters running out like spider webs in all directions. She hit it again and again and it wobbled but didn't fall. She stepped back. Was it shatterproof glass? Acrylic?

Leah bent into a crouch and hammered at the same spot with the tire iron, hitting again and again until she chipped an inch-wide hole in the window. She stuck the tire iron in the hole and pulled. The glass wobbled and bent and Leah worked enough of it loose to scramble through the hole. She pulled her duffel through, tossed it and the tire iron on the floor, and sucked in some air.

5:51.

Her whole body trembled and shook with fear and adrenaline, but she couldn't rest. She had to close the hole.

Leah cleared the bookcase one shelf at a time, using both her hands like shovels. Books fell all around her feet in heaps, self-help guides to live her best life. Another time, she would laugh at the irony, but now, with her hair half out of her ponytail and sticking to her sweaty cheeks, all she could do was push on.

When the shelves were clear, Leah grabbed the side of the bookcase farthest from the broken window and pushed. It moved an inch.

"Come on!" she screamed in frustration, and tried again. The bookcase slid half a foot. Leah paused to push sweat and hair off her face. *I have to do this. I will do this.*

Gripping the side of the bookcase again, she shoved with all her remaining strength and the bookcase slid across the floor. It hit the wall and she ran around to the back, pushing it in an arc to stand in front of the open window.

She stepped back in relief and sucked in breath after breath. It covered the hole.

Would it be enough? Would it protect her from the fallout? She didn't have a clue. She looked around her at the hundreds of books on the floor and scooped them up, adding them to the spaces around the bookcase as filler. If small amounts of air could penetrate the cracks between the bookcase and the broken glass, the books might stop it.

Leah ran back to her bag, grabbed it and the tire iron,

and hurried through the store, passing the coffee shop in the middle, the tables lined with gifts, and tucked herself into a corner. With solid walls on two sides and a bookshelf stuffed to the gills in front of her, Leah felt as safe as she could be.

She sagged to the floor, heaving and panting.

As the adrenaline seeped from her body, her teeth began to chatter. Her arms and legs shook. *I'm going into shock.* Her body was shutting down to keep her alive. She glanced at her watch.

6:01. *Thirty minutes since the blast, at least.* There was no leaving the bookstore now. She would be there until she deemed it safe to go outside. But when would that be?

What had Andy said? Two weeks? She looked around her in a panic. What would she eat? How would she keep herself warm?

Sitting on the floor, Leah couldn't see more than a few feet in either direction. The light from outside grew increasingly dimmer. Was that fallout? Cloud cover? She shivered. She couldn't stay there on the floor all night with no light and nothing to keep her warm.

Leaving her bag on the floor, she stood up and walked toward the middle aisle. Bookstores always kept their gifts in the middle. She found a table full of reading lamps and ripped one open. She clicked it on and used it like a flashlight.

In the teen and children's section, she found throw blankets and pillows embroidered with characters from popular books. Leah grabbed one of each.

A bag of chocolate-covered almonds would work for dinner. In the morning, she could debate searching the rest of the store. For now, calories and warmth would do. She hurried back to the little corner and sat down.

With the book lamp clipped to a shelf in front of her, she ripped open the blanket and took the wrapping off the pillow. Never in her life had she been so thankful for the commercialization of everything. She slipped the pillow beneath her cold backside and wrapped the blanket around her shoulders.

The almonds were trickier to open, but after a handful, she stopped shaking. Snot and sweat dried across her face and she snuffed a glob of congestion down her throat. The book lamp lit up the shelves in front of her.

Military history. *Of all the luck.* She scanned the titles and froze. An entire shelf on World War II sat at eye level. Leah reached out and plucked a book from the shelf and read the title. *After Hiroshima: An Oral History of the Aftermath.*

Tears pricked her eyes and she cradled the book in her lap, unable to open it. The reality of what happened threatened to overwhelm her. A nuclear attack. Millions must be dead and countless more injured.

Her eyes overflowed and she wiped away the moisture. Crying wouldn't do her any good. But as long as she had a reading lamp, she could read. Leah settled in and opened the book. If what Andy said was true about the fallout, she had nothing but time.

CHAPTER TWENTY-ONE

GRANT

Highway 72
   South Carolina Border
   Saturday, 5:25 p.m.

Grant drove down the road with a smile on his face and the cold January wind whipping through his short hair. With not a car in sight and the beauty of nature all around him, Grant could almost forget the horror of the past day and a half.

A river came into view and the smile turned into a full-blown grin. Pushing the accelerator, Grant crossed into the state of Georgia as the sun set behind him. The gas gauge read three-quarters full and Grant had a good feeling. Everything was coming together.

With the flatter terrain and acres of pasture surrounding the road, he guessed he was close to Athens.

If all went well, he could be pulling into Hampton in an hour and a half. He hoped his wife would greet him when he knocked on her sister's door, glass of wine in hand and relief on her face.

As he glanced behind him at the red and orange sunset, a tremendous light blasted the Cutlass from the south. Grant slammed on his brakes and shielded his face with his hands. He blinked into the light, trying to find the source.

The harder he tried to focus, the more blurry everything became. Grant put the car in park and blinked to clear his vision. It was like stepping into a dark room on a clear summer day, but no matter how many times he blinked and shook his head, his vision only worsened.

All he could see was the light. Panic rose up in his throat. He slammed the car into park on gut feel of the shifter and fumbled for the door handle. The door swung open and Grant swung with it. His feet hit the asphalt and he stood, trying to see anything but the vast whiteness in front of him.

He took a step and stumbled, barely catching his balance. Another step and his foot slipped into a pot hole. Grant's hands hit the blacktop first, the bits of rock and tar scraping his skin. As his knees followed, slamming to the ground and sending waves of shock up his bones, he screamed.

I'm blind! What if it's permanent? What if my sight never comes back?

His breath caught in his throat and his chest

hammered louder than the idling car engine. He didn't know what to do. How could he reach his wife now? He was in the middle of nowhere with a full gas tank and car that could get him home, but he couldn't see to drive.

He rolled onto his side and sat up before closing his eyes against the horror. There was only one thing the flash of light could have been: a nuclear bomb.

Baker, the hacker from the tournament in Charlotte, was right. A kid with computer skills and no common sense found out what no one else could. And Grant didn't listen. Not really.

He'd been nervous and harried and made some tough choices, but he hadn't fought as hard as he could. He didn't move heaven and earth to find his wife in Atlanta. Was there anything left of the city? Did she make it out before the blast?

I'm such an idiot. He should have told her everything via voicemail instead of hedging and trying not to worry her. All he did was wreck her chances. She was so good, so kind. The caretaker part of her would want to stay at the hospital no matter what.

If she didn't leave, then she was most likely dead. Grant swallowed. Had the other bombs gone off as well? Was it a coordinated attack? Were the major cities all across the United States suffering?

Millions of people would be dead. The country would be thrust into chaos. Anarchy.

I'm at least a hundred miles from Atlanta, maybe more. Am I safe here from the fallout? Do I need to hide?

With shaky hands that still stung from the fall, Grant clambered back inside the car and shut the door. He reached beneath the steering column and found the run wires.

As he pulled them apart, he took a deep breath. This couldn't be the end. He thought positive thoughts, repeating over and over again in his mind that the blindness would fade and he would see again.

Leaning back on the seat, visions of his wife swam in the afterglow of the explosion behind his eyes. He sent up a prayer, begging for her safety.

It didn't take long for exhaustion to overtake him. Grant drifted into unconsciousness, his wife the only thing on his mind.

7:30 p.m.

His leg jerked in his sleep and Grant slammed his knee into the steering wheel of the Cutlass. He groaned and opened his eyes. The dark, blurry world swam before him as the horror of the bomb filled his mind.

He rubbed his eyes. Opened them again. *I can see!*

He whooped for joy, beating the steering wheel with both fists. *I can see!*

According to his watch, it was 7:30. Grant rushed to start the car. He didn't know where to go or what to do.

How far did radiation travel? Was it coming his way? He wished he'd paid more attention to history all those years ago.

All he could do was keep moving. Leah's sister lived close to forty miles from downtown. Fallout couldn't reach there, could it? Grant shifted the Cutlass into drive and kept heading deeper into Georgia. If he could find an open business, maybe someone there would know.

Ten miles later, the road opened up and signs appeared for a larger, divided highway heading north and south. Grant slowed the car. Taking the highway would get him closer to Atlanta. But could he risk it?

Continuing on would put him on the western side of the city and north of Hampton. He kept going. As he crossed over the highway, a parking lot full of tractor-trailers caught his eye. The signs above the gas station were dark, but he could still make out the words.

24-Hour Truck Stop
Showers, Internet, Hot Food

They didn't have power. The place was probably closed. But as Grant was about to drive past, Logan's words popped into his head. The man claimed to learn about the attack from truckers on ham radios. Grant slowed and pulled into the lot.

Twenty or so trucks were parked in extra-long spaces beside the building. If even one driver was active on a radio, maybe he could find out what happened.

A dim light glowed from inside the truck stop and as Grant eased closer, he could make out a small crowd gathered around a table. He parked in the empty car lot and opened the door. The shotgun sat on the seat beside him and Grant hesitated. He couldn't leave it, but he couldn't bring it in.

In the end, he decided to shove it in his suitcase and roll the whole thing inside. As he opened the door, bells jingled. About fifteen men of varying ages, most with ball caps perched on their knees, turned around. Beards. Mustaches. Tattoos up and down arms.

Truckers.

Grant nodded. "Good evening."

A few men nodded in return.

He smiled a tight smile. "I was hoping someone might know about the explosion. I've got a wife in Atlanta." His voice cracked. "I don't know if she's all right."

Faces around the table softened. One man pulled out a chair. "Come and sit. We're talking about it now."

Grant bobbed his head in appreciation and wheeled his suitcase over to the empty chair. He sat down and faced the crowd. "I'm Grant Walton. I'm from just outside of Atlanta. My wife is a nurse at Georgia Memorial."

He felt like he'd just introduced himself at an AA meeting and everyone around the table should say, "Hello, Grant." But they didn't. A few averted their eyes. A couple nodded.

One man cleared his throat. Twenty years older than

Grant at least, he sported a crew cut that spread into graying lamb chops across his jaw. As he leaned back in his chair, his cowboy boots scraped against the floor. "From what we've pieced together over the radio, we've confirmed bombs in Atlanta, Charlotte, Dallas, Houston and... where in Florida?"

Another man chimed in. "Miami, Orlando, and Tampa."

"We're not sure about anywhere else. The radio reception isn't great right now. Since truckers are almost all grounded, we're not able to chain relay the information like we usually do."

Grant wiped his face. "That's seven confirmed nuclear bombs. Anyone know the size?"

"No. Most of our contacts live outside the city. We're not big on urban living, are we, fellas?"

A smattering of no's and naw's and nu-uh's echoed back.

The man nodded at Grant. "You know anything?"

"The first I heard about it was Friday at a computer convention in Charlotte. Some kid said he found evidence of an impending attack online." Grant focused on the scrapes across his palms. "The top twenty-five cities were targets, timeline unknown."

"Anything else?"

Grant glanced up. "He thought the bombs were smuggled in via container ships."

A trucker across from Grant with a Dolphins hat perched on his knee responded. "That would make sense. Those things are never checked."

"They are when they get on the ground."

"But not on the boat, you know that, Randy." The man who was the first to speak eased off his chair and leaned forward far enough to stick out his hand. "I'm Dennis. I drive long-haul Tampa to Pittsburgh."

Grant shook his hand and the man next to him spoke up. He was about Grant's age, with sandy blond hair and a friendly smile. "Bill. I'm Atlanta to Memphis."

The man with the Dolphins hat spoke up, his face tanned and wrinkled by years in the front of a cab. "Travis. Miami to Chicago."

Each man around the table introduced themselves, one after the other, with their name and what route they usually drove. Grant smiled and shook each offered hand. "Good to meet you all. I wish it were under better circumstances."

"Your wife's in Atlanta?" Dennis shook his head. "You know it's not good, right?"

Grant nodded. "I sent her a million messages and texts and told her to go to her sister's in Hampton. That's where I hope she's at."

"Are you headed that way?"

"I am, as soon as I figure out whether it's safe. I don't want to drive all that way only to get sick."

"From the fallout."

Grant nodded. "I don't know much about it, but I remember talking about it in school. How it's invisible, so you don't know you've been exposed until you get sick."

Randy cleared his throat. "Before you came in, I was

sharing what I know. I could start over if the rest of the group doesn't mind."

A rush of "*go aheads*," spread through the group and bodies shifted to get more comfortable. Randy pulled out a book.

CHAPTER TWENTY-TWO

GRANT

Highway 72
   South Carolina Border
   Saturday, 8:30 p.m.

"Mind you, some of this stuff is a bit dated, and maybe overkill, but I figure we're in a new world now. We should know all we can."

Randy flipped the pages on a worn textbook with beat-up corners and highlighting on every page. He pulled a pair of reading glasses from his shirt pocket and leaned forward. "At the height of the Cold War, there were about sixty-five thousand nuclear weapons available to be used."

Grant blinked. *Sixty-five thousand?* He remembered the stories about the 1950s when people built fallout shelters in their basements and stocked a year's supply of food in case they couldn't come up to the surface, but that many bombs?

"Globally, now we're down to about fifteen thousand weapons that haven't been decommissioned."

A trucker from across the table spoke up. "What's that mean?"

Randy scratched behind his ear. "Different things to different countries. For us, it means the bombs were dismantled. For Russia, it could mean they were abandoned in warehouses in difficult climates with little protection."

"You mean they aren't guarded?"

"That's exactly what I mean. According to some recent surveys, there are one to two thousand metric tons of enriched uranium available in the world. At least one hundred of those metric tons are very insecure."

"How much is in a bomb?"

"The bomb dropped on Hiroshima only needed about seventy-five pounds of enriched uranium."

"You're joking."

"Not one bit. The uranium needed would take up as much space as about eight cans of Coke."

Grant swallowed. Someone only needed to smuggle in eight cans of Coke to blow up an entire city. It didn't seem real. "Who knows how to make these bombs?"

"Anyone with access to the internet and a science degree could probably do it."

Bill spoke up. "That light we saw was pretty bright. Keith looked at it and he's still seeing spots."

Grant nodded. "Same here."

Randy frowned. "You'll need to watch your vision. Looking at the blast is one of the worst things you could have done. You might be able to see now, but it might not last."

Grant leaned back in his chair. He knew staring at the sun could blind him, so why had he stared at the explosion? He rubbed his eyes. Leah would never forgive him if he lost his sight... If she was still alive.

He looked back up. "Say the bombs are the size you mentioned, like in World War II. What kind of damage are we talking about?"

Randy flipped a few pages in the book. "Ninety percent fatal within a half mile of the blast site. Whoever was outside in the immediate vicinity would be vaporized. The explosion is unimaginably hot."

"Beyond that?"

"Two miles out, there would be incredible damage to buildings with hurricane force winds. Almost total destruction, collapsed high-rises and overpasses, shattered windows. Nothing would be left standing. Most people within two miles would die from their injuries or burns from the blast."

Grant thought about Georgia Memorial. It sat within two miles of the state Capitol, he was sure of it. If Leah stayed at work and didn't leave for her sister's place, there was a strong likelihood she was dead.

He pinched the bridge of his nose. *I have to have faith.* Leah made it out of the city. She was with Dawn right now, worrying about him. She had to be.

Randy flipped another page. "Up to eight miles out,

people would have twenty minutes to thirty minutes to take cover until the mushroom cloud fallout would start falling back to earth."

"That's it? I thought it was an hour?"

Randy nodded at Travis. "It depends on the size of the cloud and the prevailing winds. But the fallout area can be as wide as twenty miles in the first twenty-four hours."

Grant focused on his hands. "What happens if you're outside in the fallout?"

"Depends on how much exposure and when. If you're outside when the first fallout comes back to earth and you stay outside, you'll die pretty soon. But radiation can be washed off. It's invisible to us, but the fallout is really just radioactive dust. If you get inside, change your clothes and take a shower, you have a chance to survive."

Randy flipped another page. "If you're exposed to a less than lethal dose, you'll suffer from radiation sickness but you may survive. If you do, you'll probably get cancer later, but the bomb won't kill you outright."

"Can the fallout come here?"

Randy nodded. "If the winds are strong enough, yes. It'll take two weeks for the radiation to decay enough to not be harmful. In the meantime, the dust will spread via wind."

"So if we're in the path of the plume next week, we could still get sick?"

"Yep. Best bet is to monitor the wind direction and stay well clear of any plume. That or stay inside."

Grant was overwhelmed. He leaned back in his chair

and closed his eyes. If the blast didn't kill Leah, the resulting fallout might. Grant would probably go blind, most of the Atlanta population was either dead or dying, and he didn't know when he could leave this truck stop in the middle of nowhere.

A hand landed on his shoulder and he jerked his eyes open. Bill smiled a sad, conciliatory smile. "We're all in the same boat, my friend."

"Do you have someone in Atlanta?"

"My entire family. Wife and four kids."

Grant's mouth fell open. "I'm sorry."

Bill pointed at Travis. "His whole family's in Miami. Dennis is from Tampa. He's got three grandkids there."

"Four, if you count the one on the way."

Bill pulled his hand away. "We know what you're going through."

"When do you think it will be safe to travel?"

"Pete is out in his cab, monitoring the weather. He's got a whole little meteorology thing going out there. Weather's his thing. If the winds change, he'll let us know."

"Until then, we're hunkering down and riding it out right here."

Grant rubbed his face and took stock. Hampton was out of the immediate vicinity of the blast. Leah's sister Dawn was safe. If Leah was there, she was safe for the time being, as well, until and unless the fallout plume headed her way.

The truck stop was as good a place as any to wait it out. Ten miles from the South Carolina border and close to a hundred miles from Atlanta, it would be days before the fallout reached it. If the wind didn't shift and he stayed there two weeks, he would be guaranteed to be free from any radiation. But he couldn't do it.

Two weeks sitting on his hands, not knowing if his wife were alive or dead?

He'd rather drive straight to the heart of the city and find her charred remains than stay there in the dark. Grant exhaled. No matter how much it pained him, he would have to wait until he had more information.

As he sat there agonizing over all the what-ifs, the front door opened. Another trucker stepped inside with a spiral notebook in one hand and a beer in the other.

Dennis spoke first. "Give us good news, Pete."

"The wind's headed due east at about ten miles an hour. Assuming it stays constant, the fallout will spread over the next week straight from Atlanta to the coast. Everything on the west side of the city should be fine."

"What about north?"

Pete gave an encouraging nod. "Assuming the wind doesn't change, it should be fine. We'll know more tomorrow."

Grant leaned back in relief. Hampton sat due northwest from Atlanta. If the winds stayed in this direction, Dawn would be fine and he could head there soon.

Bill motioned to the back of the store. "We've got working showers. The heat's natural gas and it's still running, too."

Grant glanced at his suitcase. "Any chance the washers work?"

"Nope. But there's an oversized sink. You could scrub up your clothes by hand and hang them on the line."

"Thanks." He turned to face the group. "I appreciate all of you letting me stay and listen. I needed to hear it."

Dennis nodded. "Anytime. Most of us are sleeping in our berths tonight, but you're welcome to a bench in the restaurant. Might be warmer than that old beater out there."

Grant smiled. "She's not a beater. She's a classic."

Dennis shook his head. "I'm more of a Caddy man, myself."

"Oh, don't get me started." Bill leaned back in his chair. "It's Ford all the way."

"You mean one of those found-on-roadside-dead things?" Travis grinned. "Chevy's where it's at."

Grant laughed and pushed out of his seat. At least in the face of uncertainty, these men still had their sense of humor. He wheeled his suitcase toward the showers and exhaled. At the most, he'd wait a few days.

Then he could find his wife.

CHAPTER TWENTY-THREE

LEAH

Barnes & Noble
 Greater Atlanta Area
 Saturday, 9:00 p.m.

Leah smacked the book lamp as it flickered in and out. Ever since opening the book about Hiroshima, she'd barely moved enough to blink. So far, she'd learned all about nuclear weapons and what to expect in the immediate aftermath.

It was horrible. Every sentence made her thankful for the Barnes & Noble and the tire iron in the back of the Buick.

If the window hadn't given way at last, or she hadn't made the right onto the larger road and come across the bookstore, she would be dead or dying. For people exposed to the blast, those close enough were incinerated. Those within two miles were burned worse than any sunburn, some even imprinted with the patterns on their clothes.

She thought about Georgia Memorial. Kelly and Stacy and all those babies. Even if they survived the heat, the building could never withstand the force of the explosion. The concrete would crumble and every patient and nurse and doctor would die.

Leah closed the book and sucked in a breath. Her heart ached for her friends and her coworkers. A flood of more tears filled her eyes and she squeezed the bridge of her nose until they passed. The remaining headache forced her eyes open.

If she hadn't left with Andy in the morning, she would be dead. Turned to dust or vapor and Grant would never know. He would never find her body.

Wiping at her blurry eyes, she opened the book again. After explaining the blast, the author moved to the mushroom cloud. Made of vaporized particles of earth from the crater caused by the bomb, the cloud was full of radiation. Within thirty minutes after the blast, those particles began to fall back to earth.

The first two days were the most dangerous. She read about how radiation is measured in absorbed radiation doses, or rads. At sufficient exposure, a person's hair would fall out, followed by a reduction in blood cell count. Nausea and vomiting would soon follow. It was a gruesome and unpleasant way to die.

Did Andy make it into the basement? What about so many of his neighbors? She thought about Becky and Tom, and all the other people she didn't even meet. Did

Andy's little dogs, Tinker and Bell, get left in the cold January air to suffer radiation poisoning?

Leah looked down at her skin. *I wasn't outside for long enough to be exposed, was I?* The book outlined ways to minimize exposure and she pored over the details. Decontamination worked: changing clothes and taking a shower actually reduced exposure.

She shrugged off the blanket and threw it away before grabbing her duffel and rushing to the coffee shop sitting in the middle of the bookstore. *Better safe than sorry.*

Grabbing another book light, she clipped it to the edge of the sink before stripping out of her clothes. She dumped them all in the sink, filled the basin with water, and added a heavy dose of dish soap. As the cold from the tile floor seeped into her bare feet, she grabbed her dirty shirt from inside her duffel and soaked it in water and soap. Using it as a sponge, she cleaned her skin as best she could, dripping and splashing water all over the tile.

Leah hesitated with her hair, since she was already shivering and chattering in the cold air. But she didn't have a choice. If vaporized bits of radioactive particles were all over her clothes, they were in her hair, too. With a pitcher of water and even more soap, she washed her hair, dunking her head in the water again and again until fresh water ran clear.

Her fingers fumbled with the clothes as she agitated the water. Leah tried to scrub them with her hands, but she couldn't get a grip. *Come on, Leah. Don't get hypothermia.*

As she rubbed her bare arms to warm up, Leah scampered back to the blankets and grabbed a new one. Her toes were numb, her fingers barely worked, but it was worth it. A cheap blanket from a bookstore never felt better as Leah wrapped it around her shoulders.

She waited until the feeling came back to her fingers before heading back into the kitchen and rinsing her clothes. Staring at the wet heap in the sink, she hesitated. If she left them there, they would never dry. But it wasn't exactly a full-service laundromat.

There has to be something.

Leah grabbed the book light and spun around. She spied an extension cord looping around the back off the now-worthless refrigeration unit and pounced on it. Fifteen feet long, it would do the trick. Looping it around one of the handles to the display cabinet showing off stale muffins and hard croissants, Leah stretched it across the tile to the opposite side. She looped it around the iron railing separating the coffee shop from the rest of the store and tugged to make sure it would hold.

One by one, Leah hung up her clothes. She smiled at a job well done. *Radiation gone. Decontamination complete.*

Before heading back to the far corner of the store, Leah grabbed the book light, a muffin, and a bottle of water. She opted for a spot one row over from where she'd been before in case she tracked radiation into that area.

As she eased herself down, reality hit her. She was

alone in a bookstore with no one to talk to and barely any food. The water still worked, but for how long?

She glanced up at the dark all around her. *Can I really stay here two weeks? Can I wait that long to find my family?*

Dawn must be worried sick. Even in Hampton, she would have seen the blast. They would have to know about the explosion, even if they didn't know what caused it. Leah's eyes went wide. What if her sister tried to find her? Leah hoped her husband was there to calm her down and keep her home.

She knew she should sleep, but worry propped her eyelids open. Wrapping the blanket tighter around her shoulders, Leah wandered back out of the aisle and took stock. Children's books, art history, architecture. *Travel.* Leah paused.

Travel would have maps. Maybe she could plot a way out that would give her an early chance. If she could find a way out of the bookstore where she wouldn't run the risk of radiation exposure, she could leave.

Exhaustion tugged at her eyes, but she fought it off and found the shelf stuffed with maps. Leah pulled out every map of north Georgia and Atlanta before heading back to her little cave.

She didn't know if leaving early would be possible, but she could at least try to figure it out. She could sleep tomorrow.

Tonight, I'm making a plan.

CHAPTER TWENTY-FOUR

GRANT

Highway 72
  South Carolina Border
  Wednesday, 10:00 a.m.

Three and a half days of being cooped up in a dark building with over fifteen truckers would drive anyone insane. Grant sat beside Pete in the cab of his eighteen-wheeler, going over the readings again.

The whole truck was outfitted like a beach in southern California with ocean blue walls and a surfboard shine to the dash. But the chill vibe did nothing to ease Grant's anxiety.

He ran a hand over his newly growing beard. "Are you sure it's safe? I can head to Hampton?"

Pete huffed out a breath and turned to him. "Dude. I've been over this like eighty times. The winds have stayed constant and are headed east. The plume is spreading toward the coast. Hampton is in the clear."

"How far south can I go?"

Pete hesitated. "I wouldn't stray nearer than twenty-five miles. Maybe thirty."

It didn't give him much to work with, but at least he could find out if Leah was safe and at her sister's. Grant nodded. "Thanks, Pete."

"You're welcome. Now get out of my cab before you totally wreck the mojo."

Grant smiled and clambered down to the parking lot. He checked the time. The guys inside had just started their morning reach-out to other ham radio operators. Grant hurried inside to listen.

The bells jingled on the door and Bill lifted a hand for silence. Grant eased the door shut and approached the table. He stopped beside Randy, the man who shared the nuclear weapon knowledge on Grant's arrival.

A radio sat beside the window, its huge antenna anchored to the roof for better range.

"Like I said, it's bad. Charlotte's destroyed. From my window, I can't see any major buildings left standing. There are fires all over downtown. I can see the smoke in the day and the flames at night even without the scope."

Randy leaned over to whisper. "He's holed up in an apartment building outside the city. Got a sweet telescope that lets him see everything."

Dennis asked another question over the ham. "Any military presence you can see?"

"Nothing. Not a single one."

Grant frowned. Shouldn't they have mobilized by now?

Three days was enough time for the army to assemble teams and start fanning out. They would be securing the bomb sites and triaging the sick and injured. It was standard practice for any kind of attack. They drilled for that kind of mission when he was active duty.

Would lack of phones really make that much of a difference? Military bases had radios and EMP-hardened equipment. Some Humvees would have survived the EMP. Fort Bragg was two and a half hours from Charlotte. Soldiers should be in the city already.

He paused. Unless they were told to wait because of radiation.

With all the testing from the Cold War, the military would know when it was safe to enter a hot zone. If the people now sick with radiation poisoning were going to die no matter what, he could understand the wait. It wasn't the humanitarian choice, but it was the sensible one. Keeping soldiers from getting sick meant more men to fight. For all Grant knew, America could be at war.

But two weeks was a long time to wait.

Healthy people would begin to panic. There would be chaos and bedlam in the streets. He couldn't imagine the horror of the major cities. Outside the blast radius, people would be alive, but desperate. Dwindling food supplies, scarce water. No electricity or information. So many cell phones with dead batteries or no signal.

He had to get to Hampton and find his wife. Grant

leaned closer to Randy. "How long before radiation symptoms manifest if someone were close to the blast?"

"Depends on the dose." Randy glanced up at the ceiling, trying to remember. "A mild dose would bring on nausea and vomiting within forty-eight hours, followed by headache and weakness. More severe exposure would speed up the timing. A large dose could bring on vomiting within the hour, along with dizziness and disorientation."

Grant ran through the timeline in his head. "So the people exposed to enough to kill them are already sick."

Randy hesitated, pulling Grant away from the radio to not disturb anyone listening. "Many are, but not all. Lower doses, or doses over a prolonged period of time will lead to bone marrow destruction and death of internal cells that regenerate quickly."

This was way out of Grant's comfort zone. He wished his wife were here to explain it to him. "Like what?"

"Your intestines, for starters. When they're damaged or killed by radiation, they don't replicate, so the GI tract doesn't heal itself. You can die of sepsis or anemia or a million other complications."

"If the radiation doesn't kill you right away, you die from its side effects?"

"Yep. For some complications, it could take months."

"Like going blind."

"Exactly."

Grant pinched the back of his neck. He had to find out if Leah was okay. If she had been exposed to a high amount of radiation, but made it to Hampton, she would already be sick. One look at her and he would know.

He thanked Randy and retreated to the bench he'd claimed as his makeshift home. With Pete's determination that the road was clear to reach Hampton, and the word from Charlotte that the cities were falling apart, Grant made up his mind.

He was leaving.

He packed up his suitcase and wheeled it back toward the group of truckers around the radio. He caught Dennis's eye and the man made his way over.

"Heading out?"

Grant nodded. "I appreciate you letting me stay here and share in your food and all the knowledge."

"That's what people do." Dennis stuck out his hand and Grant shook it. "You head back this way, stop in and see if we're still here. Most of us won't be leaving until the two weeks are up."

"Will do." Grant waved at the rest of the crowd and headed out to the Cutlass. It sat right where he left it, all alone in the car parking lot.

He stared out at the trucks that would probably never start again. They were lucky to all be there, taking a load off from the drive when the power went out. If not, who knows where they would have been. Driving smack through the middle of a major city, most likely.

Grant put his suitcase in the back seat and slid in behind the wheel. He tapped the starter wires together and the Cutlass sputtered to life. As the car backed out of the space, Grant exhaled. *I'm coming, Leah. Just hold on.*

He headed due west, following the handwritten map Bill had drawn on a scrap piece of paper. The farther he traveled, the more surreal it all became.

He passed little farm houses with white clapboard siding and black shutters. A double-wide with a dog house out front and a five-year-old kid kicking a ball in the gravel driveway. A horse grazing along the fence line. Cows in the distance.

How would everyone survive without power? Would the water keep running in the taps? Would the gas stay on? There was so much Grant didn't know.

So much uncertainty and fear. The nuclear detonation consumed his thoughts for the past two days, but out in the country, other fears surfaced. Dawn lived in a small town where everyone knew each other and nothing was secret for long.

How would they be getting on, three days without power?

Grant increased his speed, worry and anxiety spurring him on. He dodged a handful of cars abandoned in the road before turning to head north to Hampton. Forty miles outside of Atlanta, it was more a little town that got swallowed up by expansion than satellite suburb for the well-to-do.

It didn't take more than half an hour to reach the city limits. With a population of a little over twenty thousand, Hampton's main drag housed the county courthouse, a string of strip mall lawyers, and a couple of restaurants that didn't try to be hip.

Grant eased onto Main Street and slowed. An old

Georgia red brick building with boarded-up windows took up the entire first block. Chain-link construction fencing blocked it off with signs proclaiming, *Your tax dollars at work! Restoration in Progress!*

Grant snorted. Not anymore. A gazebo with a historical marker sat in the middle of a manicured lawn in front of the old courthouse. A gathering of people huddled together beneath the patinated copper roof. They all turned to watch him drive by.

He stopped at the stop sign and turned left toward Dawn's street. A classic Victorian-era house sat on the corner. A child played on the front step with a toy stable and plastic horses. Grant drove past.

On the next street, Victorians gave way to 1920s craftsman bungalows and even smaller 1940s cape cods. He turned into Dawn's neighborhood with growing apprehension. People milled about outside. Neighbors chatting with other neighbors, teenage boys playing soccer in the middle of the street.

Every person turned when they heard the rumble of the Cutlass. He frowned. In a town like Hampton, he couldn't have the only working car. He'd already passed his fair share of beaters, some even older than the '77.

But he supposed he was still a novelty; a stranger.

Turning onto Dawn's street, he counted the houses. She lived in the fourth one on the right. A tiny little brick bungalow with a kelly green front door. He bounced up the driveway and came to a stop behind a ten-year-old Kia Sedona. Dawn's car.

Grant swiveled in the seat, looking for any sign of

Leah's little sedan. It wasn't there. He pulled the run wires apart, grabbed his suitcase from the back, and struggled out of the car. White curtains moved in the house next door. Grant ignored them.

He walked up to the front door, carrying his suitcase over cracked concrete steps, and took a deep breath. *This is it.* He knocked, twice.

Hurrying feet sounded inside and moments later, the door swung open. Dawn stood in the open door, looking every bit the younger version of Leah. Same blonde hair pulled back in a haphazard ponytail. Same trim figure, only an inch or two taller.

She smiled and it almost broke Grant's heart. "Grant! You're safe!" Dawn reached out and wrapped him up in a massive squeeze before pulling back.

One look at his face and Dawn's smile slipped into confusion. She rose up on her tiptoes to look behind him. "Where's my sister? Where's Leah?"

CHAPTER TWENTY-FIVE

LEAH

Barnes & Noble
    Greater Atlanta Area
    Wednesday, 10:00 a.m.

Leah sat in clean clothes, stretching behind her back to braid her own hair. Day four of living in a bookstore, and she'd run out of books on nuclear bombs, water, and edible food. Most of the coffee shop's supplies were dependent on refrigeration. Without it, everything spoiled.

She ate the last questionable muffin the morning before. There wasn't anything left. She'd even eaten the candy in the kids' section. All the little cellophane bags were in the trash and Leah didn't feel any better.

Her stomach ached and every so often her vision blurred. A headache pounded in the base of her skull. She was dehydrated and beginning to make stupid mistakes. It started with a nasty paper cut. Then she'd tripped over a stack of books and cut her knee.

Too much more and she would doubt her ability to leave. She turned and looked at the coffee shop. The water still ran, but she wasn't sure if she could trust it. One of the books outlined how water could become contaminated with radiation thanks to the invisible particles soaking into the ground and ending up in wells and treatment facilities.

The last bottle of water sat in front of her on the table. *An inch of water left.* Her lips cracked as she grimaced. *Three days.* That's about how long the human body could survive without water before suffering permanent damage. One down, two to go.

She unfolded the map of Atlanta and remeasured her route for the tenth time. According to the map, the Barnes & Noble sat approximately ten miles from the state Capitol in a straight shot to the northwest.

If she were a bird, she could fly another thirty miles and be knocking on her sister's door in time for lunch. But she wasn't. She was human and susceptible to radiation poisoning.

Her stomach rumbled.

And easily overcome by starvation.

Leah pressed her lips together. Ten miles was the very edge of typical radiation clouds for the bombs in World War II. If the one detonated in Atlanta were of a similar size, then she might be okay leaving now and heading away from the city.

If the bomb were bigger, it would be too soon.

She rested her head in her hands, unsure what to do. Waiting would kill her. Leaving too soon would kill her. She stood up in a rush and trotted to the kid's section. Enough drama and headache. Distraction worked to ease hunger pains; maybe it would work to clear her mind.

The shelves were stuffed with every picture book she loved as a kid. *Blueberries for Sal, Where the Wild Things Are, The Velveteen Rabbit*.

Leah plucked one she'd never read off the shelf and cracked it open. It told the story of a girl who came down with a bad case of stripes all because of lima beans. Leah laughed out loud at the hilarious sickness. She wished she'd known of the book when she spent a month training in the children's unit at Georgia Memorial.

One thought of the hospital and Leah shut the book.

She stared out at the sea of illustrated covers and choked back a sob. All the children and their families. All dead or dying. And for what? Why?

She put the book back and clutched her middle. Was Atlanta the only city hit? Or were the top twenty-five now home to the sick and injured and dead? How would the country ever repair itself?

Would other countries rush in to help? Was the United States at war?

She worried about food production and the federal government and the military and police. A million questions burst in her mind like popcorn in a microwave. She snorted. *A microwave. Add that to the long list of things no one will remember*.

Leah screamed and kicked at a shelf of books. Half of

them fell to the floor. She couldn't stay there. She couldn't be trapped in a bookstore and her own head, slowly dying of starvation and dehydration while the rest of world died of radiation sickness.

Grant could be in his final hours. He could be out there somewhere sucking in his last ragged breath and Leah wouldn't know. She wouldn't be there to comfort him or wipe his brow or ease his pain.

She wasn't easing anyone's suffering. Not even her own.

Leah walked over to the front windows. The Buick sat in the parking lot exactly where she left it, doors and windows shut. Could she drive without the risk of radiation? Or was the car full of it?

She checked her watch. The bomb went off around 5:30 four days ago. That put it close to ninety hours post-explosion. All the books claimed the radiation was the worst within the first seventy-two hours.

If she rushed to the car, got in and drove as fast as she could toward Dawn's place, how much radiation would she be exposed to? She swallowed. *I'll have to risk it.*

She turned around to grab her things when the room spun. She grabbed a bookcase for support. *I can't make it to Dawn's without food. I'll pass out in the car and crash.*

Leah eased back down into the chair and focused on the map. If she stayed on the road with the bookstore, she would hit a major cross-street in a mile that she could take all the way to Hampton. It wouldn't be the fastest, but it would be the least likely to be jammed with cars and the most likely to have a store.

Highways were out of the question.

There had to be a pharmacy or a grocery store on the route. Somewhere ten miles from the bookstore and well out of the range of any plume. She could stop, load up her body, and make it the rest of the way.

All she had to do was hold on long enough to find it.

CHAPTER TWENTY-SIX

GRANT

83 Iris Street
   Hampton, Georgia
   Wednesday, 11:00 a.m.

"What do you mean, she's not with you?" Dawn paced in her kitchen, one hand on her head and the other wagging at Grant. "Leah has to be with you! You're her husband!"

"I was in Charlotte at a conference. I've already explained this three times." Grant sat at the kitchen counter, barely able to contain his frustration. He should be on the road looking for Leah, not fielding the same questions over and over from her sister.

"We'll have to go looking. Do you think she's at the hospital?"

Grant jerked his head up. "There's nothing left of the hospital."

Dawn froze. "What are you talking about?"

"The bomb."

"What bomb?"

Grant tried to control his tone. "You're joking, right?"

Dawn's face turned that shade of pink Leah's became only when she was about to blow a gasket. "I don't know what kind of game you're pulling, Grant Walton, but if you don't tell me what in blazes is going on, I'm going to lose it."

The front door opened and Grant turned around. Dawn's husband Chris stood in the entry, a smile lighting up his face. "Hey, Grant! Good to see you!" He turned to his wife and the smile slipped to an open mouth. "Babe, you okay?"

"No, I am not okay!" Dawn stamped her foot. "Grant is sitting there telling me that he doesn't know where Leah is and that some bomb went off!"

Chris shut the door and walked into the kitchen. He gave his wife a squeeze before addressing Grant. "Care to explain? You've never struck me as the crazy type, but that car you're driving is a little out there."

Grant gripped the counter and leaned back. "Are you two telling me that you didn't see the fireball Saturday night? Or the mushroom cloud hanging over Atlanta?"

"Mushroom cloud?" Dawn snuggled against her husband. "He's lost his mind."

"No, I haven't." Grant pushed up to stand and ran a hand through his hair. "A nuclear bomb went off in the city Saturday around five thirty or six. From here you should have seen a flash of light and I would have thought a cloud."

Dawn looked up at Chris with a frown. "Saturday night we were all at the rec center having a community meeting. The sheriff gave us an update on the power outage."

Chris agreed. "We were there from five to about eight or nine. It's a big gymnasium. There aren't windows."

"You can't be serious." Grant clenched his fists. "You don't know. I can't believe you don't know."

"Don't know what?"

He looked up at Dawn and her husband. "The United States was attacked. The power outage was caused by a high-altitude nuclear bomb. It caused an EMP that knocked out the power across the entire eastern half of the country."

Chris frowned. "The sheriff said they didn't know yet what caused it and that they were having trouble getting in contact with Georgia Power."

"That's because they can't. It's all down. Everything. That's why cars don't work and cell phones won't make calls."

Dawn smacked Chris on the chest. "I told you the cars were a big deal." She turned to Grant. "When is it all coming back? The power? The phones?"

"Probably never."

The color fled Dawn's face. She leaned back against the counter and shook her head.

Chris rubbed the back of his neck. "What's that got to do with the explosion?"

"The theory is that the EMP was a precursor.

Something to knock the government into disarray so it couldn't prevent the real attack."

Grant kept talking before one of them interrupted again. "I can't confirm every city, but it appears the top twenty-five in the United States have been the victims of a coordinated nuclear attack."

"Nuclear bombs?"

"Detonated in each city, yes. I don't know the size or the scope or if every city on that list was hit. But I got confirmation a few days ago of Atlanta, Charlotte, Denver, Houston, Miami, Tampa, and Orlando."

Dawn began to shake. "Is there anything left? Are the cities destroyed?"

"I don't know. One man who had eyes on Charlotte said there were no high-rises left and that the mushroom cloud hung above the city for an hour after the explosion."

"Did you see a cloud?"

Grant shook his head. "I was too far away and it was too dark by the time the bomb went off."

"You've always been a stand-up guy, but this is too much." Chris took his wife's hand. "I don't believe it."

Dawn hesitated, eyes shifting back and forth between Grant and her husband.

Chris jerked on her hand. "Tell him you don't believe it either, baby."

She stared at Grant for a hard minute, but at last, agreed with her husband. "Unless you have proof, I—I think you should leave."

Grant didn't know what to say. He stared back at

Leah's sister, slack-jawed and confused. Never did he consider them not knowing. He swallowed and tried again. "When I was in Charlotte, I overhead a hacker talk about the threat. He said the bombs were smuggled in via shipping containers."

Chris let go of Dawn's hand and stepped toward Grant. "Now I know you're making it up. Hackers in Charlotte? We're not in a Friday night movie on cable."

"I know that, but I'm not crazy." Grant's voice rose. "The bomb probably went off downtown. If it did, Georgia Memorial is a radioactive crater in the ground. Leah could be dead."

Dawn shrank back. Whatever hesitation she had fled when Grant told her Leah might be dead. Horror replaced the confusion on her face. "Get him out of here, Chris."

Chris stepped forward, but Grant held up his hands. "You need to listen to me. Don't drive toward the city. Stay here for at least another week."

"You heard Dawn. You need to leave. Now."

Grant took a step toward the door. He couldn't believe Leah's sister didn't trust him. Why would he come there and make it up? "This is just the fear talking. Once you accept the truth, you'll know I'm right."

"I'll call the sheriff if you aren't out of here in thirty seconds."

Grant snorted. "On what phone?" He walked to the door. "I'll leave, but you should follow up with the sheriff, the mayor, and anyone else who might know something. This is bigger than a blackout. You need to be prepared."

He grabbed his suitcase and opened the door. "If I find Leah alive, I'll bring her here. Don't freak out if you see the car."

Dawn stood in the kitchen, her arms wrapped around her body just like Leah did when she was scared. Chris waited in the living room, watching Grant leave.

He took the steps two at a time and yanked the door to the Cutlass open so hard it almost swung back and hit him. If they didn't know where Leah was, he couldn't stay. But the doubt stung.

Would other people act the same way? Did any small town without access to radios or other communications not know what had happened?

Grant slid into the driver's seat and started up the car. He didn't know where to go or what to do. He checked the time. *Noon.* Over ninety hours after the explosion.

Could he risk a trip to the city? He glanced at the gas gauge. Half a tank. He didn't know where Leah could be or what he'd find inside the city limits, but he had to try.

His wife was out there somewhere, and she needed him. Grant put the car in reverse and eased back onto the road. Retracing his drive into Hampton, Grant ignored the stares of other residents. They could be suspicious all they wanted.

It didn't matter now. At the stop sign on the edge of town, Grant sucked in a deep breath and turned south. A sign beside the road proclaimed *Atlanta, 39 Miles.* Grant passed it and exhaled.

Hold on Leah, I'm coming.

CHAPTER TWENTY-SEVEN

LEAH

State Road 108
  Northern Georgia
  Wednesday, 12:00 p.m.

Standing at the front door to the bookstore, Leah hesitated. Once she opened the door, there was no going back. She would be out in the world, exposed to whatever radiation was still in the air.

Another wave of vertigo overcame her and she grabbed the door for support. *I don't have a choice. I have to go.*

She'd never been good at skipping meals. Combining a fast metabolism and a demanding job, Leah burned more calories than the average woman her size. If she didn't eat regularly, she passed out.

With a deep breath, she pushed the door open and headed for the Buick. It seemed so far away. The broken asphalt crunched beneath her feet and she picked up the pace, running across the rest of the parking lot.

Halfway to the car, she let out the last air from the bookstore and inhaled. The outside air didn't smell any different. A little colder, but that was all. *Am I breathing in radiation? Am I killing myself?*

Leah reached the car, threw herself and her bag inside, and slammed the door. She didn't feel any safer inside the oversized metal can. Thanks to fifty years on the road, it probably had as many holes in it as a colander. She glanced up at the bookstore. Too late to turn back now.

The car started as soon as she turned the key.

She drove in a wide arc, angling through the parking lot and onto the road. The street headed due north and Leah followed it, focusing on the blacktop in front of her. As long as she focused on the road, the waves of dizziness were manageable.

When she glanced in the rearview, the world wobbled and her stomach threatened to heave. Gagging on sticky spit, Leah scanned the buildings she passed for possibilities. More subdivisions, more side streets, nothing that would help.

Another major cross street loomed ahead. A gas station sat on the corner. She slowed as if to stop for the non-existent red light. Could she break in?

Bars covered the windows and the front door of the mini-mart. She thought about how hard it was to get inside the bookstore. Add in metal bars and Leah pushed the gas pedal. She needed somewhere easy. Across the street, a Walgreens with a drive-through took up the next parking lot, its sign that usually scrolled with sales and health alerts black and empty.

Cars occupied two parking spaces: an electric with the cord from the charging station still plugged into the port, and a five-year-old Honda. Neither would be working now. Leah stopped on the road and stared at the building. Were the owners of the cars inside? Would they let her in?

Bars covered one of the folding doors, but not the other. The exposed door tilted awkwardly in the track, like it had been forced apart and then haphazardly shoved back together. Leah glanced at the tire iron sitting atop her duffel in the passenger seat. It wasn't much protection.

She drove on.

The strip mall just past the pharmacy housed a restaurant and a clothing boutique and a business aimed at helping kids with math. None of them were viable.

With every rejected option, Leah's frustration grew. Driving straight to Dawn's became more and more attractive. She could make it in a couple hours if the roads were mostly clear. But what if she couldn't? What if she met an obstacle she couldn't avoid?

If she were stuck on the road until dark with no food and no water, it would be bad. She might pass out or do something stupid.

No. I need to eat.

Leah pushed on, eyes focused on the side of the road. A Waffle House sat tucked between a car wash and an apartment complex. Leah brightened. If anywhere were still open and serving food, it would be a Waffle House. As she slowed to turn in, a large, handwritten sign caught her eye.

We Are Out of Food!
Closed Until Further Notice!

Leah sank in the seat. Of course they were out of food. With the blackout hitting a day before the bombs, the place probably ran out of food within a single shift. Without a freezer, what they couldn't cook would go bad before the day was out.

Trapped in the hospital, working to keep patients alive, Leah hadn't experienced the full onslaught of the EMP. She missed the initial confusion and the run on the stores. Most supermarkets were probably raided with panicked neighbors buying bread and water and everything else they could get their hands on.

She would be lucky if anywhere had anything left. A wave of dizziness and panic gripped her, but she pushed ahead, coasting around a gaggle of stalled cars and on down the road.

Five miles later, Leah spotted it. An overgrown shrub camouflaged half of the sign, but the bright blue and yellow still showed through. *Walmart.*

If anywhere were still open, it would be a super center. Most stayed open twenty-four hours. And what were the chances a place that big was out of food already?

Leah turned into the parking lot and eased over the speed bumps.

About fifteen cars sat in the parking lot, abandoned from the looks of them. She cruised up to the front doors, ready to park along the side of the building when her breath caught in her throat.

Glass littered the concrete. A flipped-over shopping cart wedged between the sliding doors and kept them open. Leah frowned. She wasn't the first to have this idea.

She eased up on the brake and the car rolled ten feet before she stopped. The massive store was her best option for food. It meant risking exposure to not just radiation, but whoever was inside.

Leah put the car in park and turned off the engine. There were so many unknowns. Dawn could be hurt or already suffering from radiation sickness. Her husband could be dying. The way to Hampton could be impassable.

I need food and water. I don't have a choice.

Opening the driver's door, Leah pocketed the keys and picked up the tire iron. She gripped it tightly in her hand as she approached the store. No lights on inside. Total darkness. She paused five feet from the entrance.

Fear pulsed in her veins and goosebumps rose in a wave across her skin.

Leah took a deep breath and eased through the broken front door. Twenty paces inside, with darkness closing in all around her, she stopped. Some part of her had hoped despite the broken front door that the store would be open. That one brave employee was still helping people get what they needed.

But she was also naïve and stupid. The store was closed and the knocked-over display shelves for sodas and chips and beer were proof. Looters had already ransacked the place.

If Leah wanted to eat, she would have to steal. It hadn't seemed so wrong at the bookstore. She was trapped in there, surviving nuclear fallout. It was eat the muffins that were about to go bad or starve.

But now? Now she was free to make other choices. The whole country opened up ahead of her and with a half a tank of gas, she could reach Hampton. She stood in the Walmart because she was hungry and tired and weak.

She turned back to stare at the outside. All the other people out there would be making the same choice soon. If FEMA or the military or some organized charity still in operation didn't show up soon, the millions of people sitting in their apartments and houses all around this community would be faced with the same choice.

Steal or starve.

Leah didn't want to starve. She had to believe she could stay alive. That's what she built her life on: doing all she could to save a life. Giving up now would be pointless.

With a deep breath, she walked toward the checkout. A row of pocket flashlights hung on a hook and Leah grabbed one and turned it on. Using the light, she crossed the store, heading for the boxed goods and sports drinks.

It didn't take her long to find them. With the

flashlight gripped in her teeth and the tire iron shoved in the back of her pants, Leah reached up for a twelve-pack of Gatorade. It slid off the shelf and she huffed with the weight. As she turned around, the flashlight lit up the end of the aisle and three men came into view.

Leah froze. Each one of them stared at her like she was a skittish deer in their sights. Saliva dribbled over the flashlight between her teeth and she sucked it back.

I am such an idiot. When she'd seen the broken entrance, she knew the store had been ransacked, but as soon as she found a flashlight, she forgot all about it.

One man stepped forward and Leah jerked her head to capture his entire frame in the light. He lifted a hand to shield his eyes, but Leah still caught the dried blood crusting beneath his nose and the bare patch of skin on his head.

She thought about the effects of radiation sickness that she'd learned about in the bookstore. Burns and spontaneous bleeding. The man was sick, maybe dying.

He nodded at her. "Looks heavy. Need some help?"

Leah shook her head and the flashlight beam bounced back and forth.

Another man spoke up. "See? I told you she was just a thief."

Oh, God. Why had she been so reckless? Leah took a step back. She couldn't talk with the flashlight in her mouth, but she wasn't about to spit it out.

The closest man stepped forward again. "I think she's just scared, that's all. Ain't that right, sweetheart?" He held up his hands. "There's nothing to be afraid of. We're friendly, aren't we, fellas?"

A murmur of agreement pulsed through the other two. Leah didn't know what to do. She'd dealt with combative patients and angry loved ones countless times, but she'd never really been in danger. She was a nurse and they had to listen. Eventually, her position of authority would win out.

But here, in the middle of a store aisle, she wasn't anything but an average woman with arms straining against the weight of the drinks in her arms. She could drop the drinks and run, but they might catch her. She could agree to whatever they wanted and give up. She could try and fight her way out with the tire iron.

None were suitable options.

Leah tilted her head and eased the flashlight from her mouth. With her chin, she wedged it in between the lids of two bottles. The circle of light aimed high, but lowering the case of Gatorade, she could still see the men blocking the aisle.

She knew what she had to do. It had always been the only choice. She cleared her throat. "You look sick."

The man in front wiped at the blood under his nose. "What's it to you?"

"I'm a nurse. I can help."

CHAPTER TWENTY-EIGHT

GRANT

State Road 205
    Northern Georgia
    Wednesday, 3:00 p.m.

Grant watched the gas gauge with increasing trepidation. Without a map, driving backroads north of the city was like running through a giant corn maze. Every third street was a dead end, whether from cars blocking the road or poor signage. He'd wasted plenty of gas and time.

All he could think about was whether the hospital survived the attack. If the bomb went off south of downtown, maybe it had a chance. He needed to find out where the bomb detonated. He needed a view of the city.

Grant looked around. For miles, he'd been driving past fields and farmland intermixed with brand-new subdivisions and strip malls. None of the gas stations were open. None of the businesses appeared viable.

He didn't know the area. He barely knew how to make it home.

Grant paused.

Home! Why hadn't he thought of it before? If his wife wasn't trapped downtown and she wasn't at her sister's place, maybe she went home. Their house was seventeen miles via surface street from the hospital, probably twelve or thirteen as the crow flew.

Pete had cautioned him against coming that close to the blast, but Grant had to know. He couldn't wait another week to find out if his wife was safe. They lived in a little neighborhood called Smyrna, in one of those new construction, cookie-cutters.

It wasn't their dream house, but it was affordable. The thing that sold them on it was the view. On a clear night, they could walk out onto their balcony and see all of Atlanta stretched before them. It was breathtaking.

Grant turned on the first major street he came to. If he angled toward the southeast now, he would eventually hit the perimeter highway circling the city. From there, he could navigate home.

An hour later, signs for 285 began to appear. Grant followed them until he reached an area he recognized. Half a mile ahead, an overpass spanned the highway. Grant's heart picked up speed. From the bridge, he could see downtown.

He sped up, ignoring the red line hovering just above the E on the gas gauge. The Cutlass rumbled up the hill. Grant stopped at the top and got out. He walked over to the sidewalk and the chain-link fence with barbed wire to prevent jumpers.

The sky stretched out for miles with not a cloud in it. In the near distance, he recognized the financial district of Buckhead with its high-rises covered in names of banks and titans of finance.

Not so important now.

He turned to the south and squinted into the distance. Downtown should be there. He should see the familiar spire of the Bank of America building and the round stick of the W. The two towers of the 191 Building.

Am I looking in the wrong place? Using his hand to shield against the setting sun, Grant scanned the horizon. He froze. A building he recognized stood all alone, looking like a monster bit a chunk from the middle.

The tallest building in midtown had a green pointed roof and gold tip. He'd worked there years ago when computer firms still occupied the space. It was the only building left. Grant swallowed. Downtown and midtown were destroyed. Any hope of finding Leah there was gone.

Grant slid down to the ground, parking his feet in the road and his butt on the sidewalk. It was really true. It really happened.

All this time, despite the flash, the reports on the ham radio, and the hackers from the conference, he'd held onto a shred of hope. Maybe it wasn't real. Maybe the bombs were small and not so deadly.

But they were all that and more. The heart of

Atlanta was destroyed. Were all the other major cities the same? Were other people risking a trip to see the devastation? He thought back in time. Four days since the explosion. Four days since America changed forever.

He closed his eyes and rubbed them. How would he find Leah out there? He only had one place left to look. *Home.*

Grant opened his eyes and braced to stand when movement caught his eye. A blur of something gray and furry darted behind the only car abandoned on the overpass. He watched as a set of little paws made their way around the far side of the vehicle.

He heard scrabbling and two of the paws disappeared. Was it trying to get inside? Was it hungry? Hurt?

Grant fished in his pocket and pulled out his last bit of food. A half-eaten peanut butter energy bar. He unwrapped it. The little feet froze.

He tore a small piece off and tossed it as far as he could into the road. After a minute or two, the little feet moved. A small dog, about twenty or thirty pounds at most, padded into the road. It stopped ten feet from the bit of food and twenty feet from Grant.

Covered in matted gray hair, the dog had obviously been on its own a while. It paced back and forth, unsure what to do. Grant gave a little *click, click* with his tongue and teeth, encouraging it.

He didn't know what he was doing. If the dog was sick, he shouldn't give it the last of his food. If it were owned by someone nearby, he should leave it alone. But Grant couldn't. It was hungry. Probably thirsty, too.

Grant tore off another little piece and threw it toward the animal. It bounced to a stop two feet closer than the first piece.

The dog sniffed the air and darted out. It snarfed the first piece, eyes always up and watching Grant. After a moment, it came forward and snatched the second.

Every time the dog finished, Grant threw another piece until it was within touching distance. He held the last chunk of energy bar in his hand. Up close, the dog's blue eyes were mesmerizing. It constantly watched him, darting back and forth on the road, looking for a reason to run.

Grant held out the food in his palm. The dog stopped moving. It stood three feet way, waiting. Grant smiled. He had more patience than a hungry animal. Maybe it was the years spent hunting up in a tree, waiting for a sign of a deer or turkey. Or maybe it was the latest job where he'd walked up and down aisles of computer tournaments, observing for hours.

It took ten minutes, but hunger won out and the dog came closer. Its mouth hovered an inch above Grant's palm before it snatched the rest of the energy bar and darted back a handful of paces.

As the dog gulped down the food, Grant took a chance. "You can come home with me, if you like. There will be more food. Water, too."

The dog didn't run.

Grant eased up to stand and walked over to the

Cutlass. He opened the door. "It's old, but comfortable. You can ride up front with me."

The dog stared at the car and Grant, undecided.

"Take it or leave it, but if I'm being honest, I don't like your chances on your own." Grant waited beside the car.

The dog backed up a step and Grant's insides twisted. For some reason, he wanted the dog.

"I can be kind of a jerk, but I know how to share. Whatever I have, you get some, too."

Grant glanced up at the sun. It dipped low toward the horizon. He couldn't stay on that overpass forever. He tensed to move when the dog surprised him.

It loped over to the open door, hesitated for a moment, and jumped in. It turned around three times on the passenger seat before settling down in a curled-up ball. Grant smiled and eased into the driver's seat.

"You made a good choice, my friend." He started the car and put it in drive. "Let's go home."

CHAPTER TWENTY-NINE

LEAH

Walmart
   Northern Georgia
   Wednesday, 5:00 p.m.

"Ouch! That hurts."

Leah smiled at the man wincing beneath her touch. The big ones were always softies underneath. "If I don't clean it, you'll get an infection."

She dabbed the wet cloth on the wound before slathering it in triple-antibiotic ointment. "How close were you to the blast?"

He thought it over. "Five miles, maybe."

"And how long were you outside?"

"I don't know." He scratched at a section of scalp where he'd lost a chunk of hair. "An hour, hour and a half. I picked up Howie before we ran into Dale and headed up here."

Leah nodded. From what she remembered, an hour and a half outside within the medium-impact zone meant exposure to near-lethal levels of radiation. It all came down to dose.

"Sorry we were jerks when we first saw you."

She smiled. "It's okay, Paul. I understand."

"I just couldn't stand the thought of anymore thieves, you know?" Dale walked over and sat down on a portable stool he'd found in the camping section. "When we got up here and saw the doors smashed all to bits, Paul and I jumped out and made sure it was safe. Ain't nobody gonna rob my Walmart while I've still got a job."

Leah shook her head. A group of law-abiding men keeping guard over a Walmart. It wasn't the stuff of horror movies, that's for sure. She refused to share all the terrible thoughts that flashed through her mind when she first saw them. "I thought you were going to kill me."

Paul grinned. "Did ya, really?" He reached out and jabbed Dale with a soft right hook. "See that, Dale? She thought we were mean."

"Meaner than a pair of toothless gators, that's for sure." Howie pulled up a chair and joined in the conversation. He pointed at Paul. "How's he doin'?"

Leah thought it over. "Not too bad. The burns are all first and second degree, so they should heal with enough ointment and time."

"What about his hair? It's fallin' out all over the place."

She hesitated. Ever since she offered up her services, Paul and the rest of the group had been nothing but sweet to her. Giving her food and something to drink, even rigging up a makeshift infirmary so she could check them all out. But she couldn't make magic.

She focused on Paul. "You've been exposed to a significant amount of radiation. I don't know how much, but based on your bloody nose and your hair loss, it's a lot."

He cleared his throat with a nod. "Will it kill me?"

"Maybe? If not now, then you'll probably get cancer in ten or twenty years."

"Shoot, if that boy lives twenty more years, it will be a miracle."

Leah smiled. "You'll have to take it day by day. That's all you can do. If you start to get sicker, if you can't eat and start throwing up, then it's not looking good. But if you get better and your nose stops bleeding, you can pull out of it."

"So, radiation sickness doesn't always kill you?"

She shook her head. "Nope. There were a large number of survivors in Hiroshima. People exposed to small doses of radiation, even those with worse burns than yours survived."

Paul exhaled in relief. "All this time, I thought I was a goner."

"Don't give up hope. That's the worst thing you can do." Leah put the antibiotic away and snuffed back a wave of emotion. "I've seen so many people survive when doctors never thought they could and every single one of them had faith they would make it."

She tried not to remember the hospital and all her

friends and coworkers. All the people who stayed behind to help even though they were exhausted and running on fumes. Guilt rose up in her chest, swimming in her lungs and threatening to pull her under.

She should have stayed. She should have helped until the very end. Instead, she left. Ran away like a...

"You did the right thing."

Leah glanced up. "What?"

"Leaving downtown when you did."

"How did you...?"

Paul shrugged. "I could see it on your face. You were thinking about your patients. The ones who didn't make it."

"And my coworkers." She wiped her nose with a tissue. "I left them all behind."

"And we're damn happy you did." Howie reached for a bottle of water and twisted it open. "I don't know the first thing about radiation sickness or treating someone with it. If you weren't here to help Paul, he'd still be thinking he's about to die."

"And now you can help other people." Dale chimed in. "Things are gonna get a whole heck of a lot worse before they get better."

Leah inhaled and pushed all the negative thoughts aside. "Thanks, guys." She leaned back in the folding chair. They were right.

If what she saw on the television was true, then the entire country was in the grips of a disaster bigger than anything anyone had ever known. Nurses would be in short supply.

Walking away from the hospital didn't just save her life. If she stayed true to herself, it would save countless others, too.

Howie held up a can of pork and beans. "Who's ready for dinner?"

They ate and talked about where they came from and where they planned to go. Leah shared about her husband and her sister and how she needed to leave soon to find them. Paul shared a photo of his niece and nephew and how as soon as they figured out a way to secure the Walmart, he'd be tracking them down in Kennesaw.

She watched his nose for signs of more bleeding all evening and when she didn't see any, her prognosis improved. Now that he had a bit of encouragement, he might pull through. Paul's survival would do a lot to ease the pain of loss Leah felt every time she thought about the blast.

The hospital was probably a vaporized hole in the ground. It would never save people again. She stifled a yawn and Paul stood up.

"We take shifts watching the front of the store at night. You should get some sleep. You'll be safe here."

Leah smiled, but it didn't reach her eyes. "Thanks, but I think I'll stay up for a while." It was one thing to treat Paul's injuries and share a meal, but fall asleep with three strange men and no one to help her?

It wasn't that long ago that they almost scared the pants off her. Leah snuggled down in the chair and pulled the blanket from the bookstore over her shoulders.

She watched as Howie and Dale cleaned up the makeshift campsite. It didn't take long for her eyelids to grow heavy.

The stress of the past four days combined with lack of sufficient food had Leah running on fumes. She shifted in the seat and sang a song to stay awake.

Sometime in the third stanza, she drifted off.

CHAPTER THIRTY

GRANT

State Road 205
Northern Georgia
Wednesday, 6:00 p.m.

Without street lights, Grant's neighborhood looked like a painted backdrop for a movie set. Nearly identical houses, one after the other, arranged in front of the sunset in the distance.

He pulled into his driveway with the gas gauge solidly on the E. He would need to find some gas before he hit the road. The dog perked up as he put the Cutlass in park and killed the engine. He smiled at the scruffy little thing.

"Come on, buddy. Time to go home." Grant opened the door and the dog hopped out.

With his suitcase in one hand, and the dog by his

side, Grant unlocked the door to his house. Stale air and the smell of garbage hit his nose and he turned his head.

No way would Leah tolerate such a stink. He knew she wouldn't be there, but hope had still clung to him like a bad piece of computer code he couldn't get rid of. Grant set the suitcase against the wall and walked down the hall.

The dog hung a few steps behind.

"It's okay, buddy. I'll get you some food." Grant stepped into the kitchen and stifled a gag. A trail of some nasty liquid oozed from the freezer compartment of his side-by-side fridge and Grant stepped over it. He fished out a half-eaten loaf of bread and a can of tuna and dumped the contents into a bowl.

He tried the tap, surprised the water still flowed. After filling another bowl, he carried both over to the edge of the kitchen and set them down. "I'll find you something better to eat tomorrow. But for now, this is it."

The dog came up and slurped half the bowl of water before attacking the fish and bread with gusto. Grant pulled a glass and a bottle of red wine from the cabinet and poured more than his share. Leah was the wine drinker in the house, but he needed something. *Anything.*

He took a gulp before stepping back over the mess and heading for the stairs. There was only one place he wanted to be. He kicked his shoes off out of habit and climbed in his socks up the stairs.

The master bedroom occupied the rear half of the second floor and Grant headed straight for it. He pushed the door open and the scent of Leah's perfume, all citrus and hope, hit him like a punch to the gut.

He swallowed another gulp of wine.

When they were about to be married and buy their first home, Grant originally wanted a little condo right in the heart of the city. Something in midtown by the park or maybe in the trendy area closer to downtown so Leah could walk to work or take the train. It was a Sunday afternoon in February, just after Valentine's Day, when Leah dragged him out to this subdivision.

He smiled at the floor as he conjured up the memory. She held her hands over his eyes and duck-walked him into the master bedroom. They stood together in the spot where he now stood alone and she pulled back her hands and showed him the world.

The entire Atlanta skyline had opened up before them, stunning in size and promise. Downtown leading into midtown, all the recognizable buildings laid out in a row. He had turned to Leah and kissed her breath away. Told the realtor waiting downstairs they would take it.

He carried her over the threshold as Mrs. Walton a month later. There had been talk of kids and family and the promise of the future in that home. So many nights spent on their balcony outside their bedroom overlooking the lights of the city. So bright and full of life.

Grant drained the rest of his drink and set the empty glass on his dresser. Where the skyscrapers of downtown and midtown used to be, nothing remained but darkness. No lights. No rising towers set off against the purples and pinks of the sunset.

Nothing except a giant hole in the ground and the specter of terror and maybe even war. Grant stood still, watching the last bit of light recede and the night claim the day. As he did, pinpricks of light began to glow red and orange in the city.

He took a step forward and palmed the sliding glass door. *Are those lights? Is there power?*

With a tremble in his hands, he slid the door open and stepped out onto the balcony. Only then did he see the truth. Not lights.

Fires.

What wasn't obliterated in the blast now burned.

He turned around in a rush and went back inside. The dog lay on the bed Grant shared with Leah, curled up on Leah's side like it knew she wasn't coming back.

Grant sat down on his side and held his face in his hands. He couldn't believe she was dead. He refused to believe it. There would be a future for the two of them together, somehow, some way.

He opened his eyes and paused. A handheld emergency radio sat on his bedside table. He never used it. It was one of those Christmas gifts he'd gotten from a coworker and promptly forgot about. Grant picked it up.

It either ran on batteries or a hand crank. Grant had never bothered to put batteries in it, so he pulled out the crank and gave it a whirl. Once the little light beside the power sign glowed green, he pulled out the antenna and turned the dial.

A robotic voice crackled to life. ".... Emergency Broadcast System. This is not a drill. Radiation has been detected in your area. Fallout shelters are denoted by yellow and black signs with the radiation symbol. Proceed to the nearest shelter and remain there until further notice. This is not a drill..."

The voice repeated the same message over and over again and Grant shut it off. Most of the fallout shelters in the city were buried under debris and dead bodies. Even if anyone had been able to find them, how would they get in?

Lying back on the bed, he slipped his hands behind his head. The dog lightly snored beside him. If Leah were there, he could forget all about the horror raging outside and pretend it never happened.

But without her, he could only stare at the ceiling. He closed his eyes and willed his body to relax.

Tonight, I'll sleep.

Tomorrow, I'll start the search for my wife.

CHAPTER THIRTY-ONE

LEAH

Walmart
    Northern Georgia
    Thursday, 7:00 a.m.

Leah rubbed her eyes and yawned. *Did I fall asleep?* She blinked her eyes open. Shafts of light filtered across the front of the Walmart and she blinked her watch into focus. *Seven in the morning?*

She sat up with a start. Howie and Dale were sprawled out on sleeping bags ten feet from her. Leah pushed her hair off her face and sat up. They were true to their word. They didn't hurt her.

Paul was nowhere to be found. *He must have the morning shift.* Leah eased out of the chair, picked up her flashlight, and found the women's restroom. After freshening up, she walked back to her chair and grabbed her duffel.

Slinging it over her shoulder, she thought about staying. Paul, Dale, and Howie were good men. They had good hearts and noble intentions. But this Walmart north of the city wasn't her home.

Grant had begged her to go to Dawn's place. She couldn't give up on that. She couldn't give up on Grant. Her husband might need her even more than Paul.

Leah smiled one last time at the two sleeping men and walked toward the front of the store. After sneaking around the shopping cart, she headed to the Buick. It sat right where she left it, ready and waiting. She popped the trunk, put her bag inside, and exhaled. *Now or never*.

"Leaving already?"

She jumped as she shut the trunk. Paul stood beside it, bandaged hands awkward at his sides.

"I need to find my family."

He nodded. "Thanks for fixing me up."

"You're welcome. Change the bandages every other day and use lots of the ointment."

"I will."

"And take the multivitamin I showed you, too."

"Yes, ma'am." He grinned before nodding at the store. "I pulled a few things I thought you could use."

Leah blinked. "Won't Dale be mad?"

Paul laughed. "Probably. But sooner or later he'll figure out he isn't getting paid and then all bets are off."

"It doesn't feel right."

"You need to eat. And you need to defend yourself." He hustled over to the front of the store and stepped through the door. A minute later, he came out laden with four plastic bags and what looked like a rifle.

"Gatorade, granola bars. A few cans of meat. Stuff that'll keep you full."

Leah took the bags. "Thank you."

Paul held onto the rifle. "This Walmart don't carry the good stuff anymore, but it's still got air rifles. It won't take down a person, but it might scare them off."

She stared at it. "I don't know how to use it."

"It's easy. Just pump and shoot." He handed it over. "It'll be good for huntin' rabbit and squirrel in the spring."

Leah grimaced. "I guess I'll have to get used to that, won't I?"

He smiled. "Squirrel tastes just like chicken."

"Thanks, Paul."

"Thank you, Nurse Leah."

She smiled and walked to the driver's side of the car. Leah slid into the seat and started the engine. As she pulled away, Paul waved.

She hoped the radiation sickness wouldn't claim a good man like him, but she had no way to know. He was one of millions right now suffering in the aftermath. She didn't know who was responsible for the attack or whether this was the beginning of war, but Leah made up her mind as she pulled onto the road.

It wouldn't change who she was or what she promised to do with her life. She was a nurse and she would help people, no matter what. A bomb wouldn't change that. It wouldn't change who she was meant to be.

The Buick bumped over the exit and Leah turned north.

Next stop: Hampton, Georgia.

* * *

Want to know how it all started? Subscribe to Harley's newsletter and receive *First Strike*, the prequel to the *Nuclear Survival* saga, absolutely free.

www.harleytate.com/subscribe

If you found out the world was about to end, what would you do?

Four ordinary people—a computer specialist, a hacker, a reporter, and a private investigator—are about to find out. Each one has a role to play in the hours leading up to the worst attack in United States history.

Will they rise to the occasion or will the threat of armageddon stop them in their tracks?

ACKNOWLEDGMENTS

Thank you for reading *Brace for Impact*. I hope you enjoyed reading the start of this new adventure as much as I enjoyed writing it. Grant and Leah will be pushed to their limits, they will work to overcome every obstacle put in their way.

For fans of my *After the EMP* series, don't worry, it's not over, merely on hold. I hope to be back later this year with more stories in that universe.

Over the past year, I've received a few reader emails when I change facts about cities or use fictitious names of streets and businesses. Although I try to be as realistic as possible, I do take liberties with regard to names, places, and events for the sake of the story (and to not ruffle real life feathers!). I hope you don't mind and can still go along for the ride.

If you enjoyed this book and have a moment, please consider leaving a review on Amazon. Every one helps new readers discover my work and helps me keep writing the stories you want to read.

Until next time,

Harley

ABOUT HARLEY TATE

When the world as we know it falls apart, how far will you go to survive?

Harley Tate writes edge-of-your-seat post-apocalyptic fiction exploring what happens when ordinary people are faced with impossible choices.

The apocalypse is only the beginning.

Contact Harley directly at:
www.harleytate.com
harley@harleytate.com

34803734R00142

Made in the USA
Middletown, DE
29 January 2019